DEADLY IRISH

ADRIAN A-J

MINERVA PRESS
MONTREUX   LONDON   WASHINGTON

ISBN 1 86106 270 2

First Published 1996 by
MINERVA PRESS
195 Knightsbridge
London SW7 1RE

Printed in Great Britain by
Antony Rowe Ltd, Chippenham, Wiltshire

DEADLY IRISH

Contents

A Cricketer's Invitation	7
The Assignment	12
Anna	22
Fears Unjustified	27
Q'd in to HH	32
Meet HH	39
Further Developments	52
Undercover Activities	72
No Smoking	79
An Acquaintance Renewed	83
Intrusion Vienna	96
Uneasy Action	99
Swansong Vienna	114
Tension	124
Winter Wonderland – St Moritz	134
Double-Cross	140
Vital Information	150
Callahan	154
Convention in Vienna	176
A Deadly Destination	184
Bombshell From Downing Street	200
Epilogue – Piracy on the High Seas	208

Chapter 1
A Cricketer's Invitation

With four punishing weeks at the British Government Secret Service Training School behind him, a refresher course, Peter Jameson returned to his London flat fit and alert. Commander Burt of Special Branch insisted on high standards of physical fitness for his field agents, and the School's team of physical fitness instructors had seen to it that when Jameson left their combat area, set deep in the desolate Norfolk countryside, he was in peak condition. Furthermore, he had been trained to use the variety of highly specialised electronic equipment necessary in modern espionage. His life, he had been told, could depend on an ability to adapt under all circumstances to what was classified as 'Natural Behaviour'. Natural behaviour, according to the top secret government pamphlet (dated 1988) which no one read, is "something only the subject can effect. It is impossible to learn other than by incorporating the same in the subject's own personality. Training methods, audio and visual, can only make the subject aware of it by correcting the subject's thought processes."

At the time Jameson had thought 'Yeah, yeah. What will they come up with next from the armchair of theory? See if it would have gotten you across the East German border at Checkpoint Charlie into West Berlin, with a cold sweat trickling down your back, as you zigzag your way through the 300 yards of no-man's land minefield (using a Q department gadget before reaching the safety of the Western zone.' But those were the early days when the practical triumphed over the theoretical.

But he'd studied the theory. And now, as Jameson stared at himself in the full-length mirror in the hallway of his Knightsbridge flat he saw reflected, approximately 73" of physically fit, slightly dissipated young man, whose eyes twinkled but critically bored into his own insolently saying, "You could use a re-fit Mister!" His mirrored twin nodded back at him in affirmation, so Jameson stuck his tongue out at it, before he resumed the conversation. "You are so right mister, not just a re-fit, but a complete re-fit. I know this will please my Navy boss." Was it conceivable, when he'd approved the Whitehall Natural Actions Directive, his chief could have had *him* in mind? "You big-headed old 'bathbun'" he told himself perfunctorily with a playful pucker of the lips, for he knew very well his principal, ex-seafarer Commander Burt, tolerated him grudgingly as a plus! Not being a regular Whitehall product, Jameson was unorthodox, and this suited the MI6 chief as a means of bucking the Whitehall structure. But, Jameson knew, Burt would have preferred his field agent find to have adopted a more acceptable dress code, on the rare occasions of visits to the 'corridors of power' with him. However, the mixture of a crash training course from MI6, plus Jameson's Air Force acquired experience, and the Continent of Europe disc jockey job he had been doing when recruited, had resulted in the production of a deadly combination, with an excellent result achieved for Burt's MI6 and Allan Dallas' CIA, on Jameson's first outing. It was an unusual mix of most senior, and most junior, in the very secret service, which Burt did not want questioned in Whitehall. This was one reason why nobody except himself and Allan Dallas knew that Peter Jameson was a name adopted for pirate radio then, but served as the perfect cover for the supernumerary field agent, now.

He went to his lounge and poured a liberal Gordons and tonic to help his thought processes. He added the ice and was slicing the lemon when a low-pitched buzz signified an arrival at the front door of the flat. He opened it to find a man dressed in a messenger's uniform holding a flat manila envelope.

"Peter Jameson?" he enquired.

"To his friends," replied Peter Jameson cautiously.

The man smiled.

"Then this is for you," he said and handed over the brown envelope.

He indicated a vacant space on the well thumbed quarto-sized sheet of paper containing a list of names and addresses, with a ball point pen, and said:

"Sign here, please."

After the man had gone Jameson sliced his lemon and then used the knife to slit open the envelope. He withdrew the contents and while downing his drink, read the short note. The note was in the neat handwriting of Commander Burt, Head of MI6 Special Branch. Jameson recognised it immediately, although it carried no signature and was on plain paper. It was brief and to the point, saying, 'Knowing you are a keen cricket fan when time allows, I thought you might care to join me for tea in the Long Room this afternoon. I shall be in my seat by 3 p.m.' It was hardly an invitation. It was an order.

Accompanying the note was a ticket admitting him to the Members Stand at Lord's Cricket Ground in St John's Wood. England were contesting Australia, for the Ashes. Peter Jameson glanced at his watch. It was 12 noon. He'd just have time to carry out his plans. He picked up the telephone and made a call. It was to Robert Fielding, the Regent Street hairdressers. He made himself an appointment and left the flat.

His first call was at a small shop in Soho which sold smart trendy suits and accessories. It was so long since he'd bought a suit that he wondered just how he'd look in one.

"Only one way to find out, that's to try a few on," a Scottish voice said in his ear.

He spun round to find a broadly smiling middle-aged assistant appraising him. He'd been looking at a light grey flannel suit with a stylish modern cut. He liked the long single vent and asked to try one in his size. It fitted him perfectly, so he decided to buy it. Next he selected a pale green shirt. Yes, these would do perfectly, he thought, and signed for the purchases. His next stop was at the shoe shop next door where he bought a pair of brown shoes. He was pleased with himself. 'I'm getting somewhere now,' he told himself as he headed west along Brewer Street, glancing interestedly at the photographs of strip artistes portrayed in the innumerable strip joints, into Beak Street and then turned right into Regent Street. It was a beautiful sunny afternoon and although he was looking forward to his afternoon at the world-famous headquarters of cricket, he was not exactly relishing two hours in a hairdressing salon. Walking quickly northwards in the direction of Oxford Circus, he considered the strange meeting Commander Burt had set up for that afternoon. Obviously he was going to be told something very important. He was not so naïve as to believe that Burt had merely invited him to be his guest at a cricket match, particularly as tickets in the Mound Stand for this particular game were obtainable only if you knew how to pull the right strings. No, something very important was going to happen, communism was quiet so Jameson sniffed terrorism – not frequently an MI6 bag! But he smiled to himself, he was not the only one who would be surprised. Wait until Robert Fielding had finished with him. He stopped when he reached the corner where Liberty's had their world-famous store, and waited for the lights to turn to green to allow him to cross to the other side of Regent Street.

Two hours later an almost unrecognisable Peter Jameson emerged from Fieldings. He had been put into the skilful hands of two of the famous London hairdresser's most expert employees, Martin and Peter. They had lightened the colour of his dark brown hair two shades and cut it much shorter. He was extremely pleased with his expensive new look. He hailed a passing taxi and headed home to change into his newly purchased outfit. And then it would be time to meet his Special Branch Chief at 3 p.m. He would just make it if he hurried.

Arriving at Lord's cricket ground that afternoon gave Peter Jameson a feeling of great Victorian grandeur. Driving along the busy St John's Wood Road, with the fifteen feet high brick walls of the cricket ground on his right he reached the famous Grace Gate. To be more accurate, two wrought iron gates with a tall ornamental pillar in the centre bearing the inscription, now beginning to wear thin with age and constant weathering:

'TO THE MEMORY OF WILLIAM GILBERT GRACE 1848-1915. THE GREAT CRICKETER.'

He drove through the gates and turned left into the car park where he left his BMW sports coupé, its white coachwork contrasting starkly with the other staid-looking occupants of the car park. Walking through the archway, and turning right, he entered the members' pavilion.

Chapter 2
The Assignment

Commander Burt was already in his seat. His bristly military moustache; short, swept-back, iron-grey hair; black jacket and pin-striped trousers not looking the least bit out of place amongst the other occupants. Peter Jameson let his eye wander over the oval green arena before he walked down the gangway to take his seat.

England were batting and before saying anything he watched the Australian fast bowler commence his thirty yard run, steadily increasing his pace until he reached the delivery crease and bowled the ball with a near perfect action. It hurtled through the air at about 90mph and pitched fractionally short of a length, it kicked, rising nastily. The England batsman groped forward, the ball snicked the outside edge of the bat and flew low and fast to first slip who dived to his right like a goal keeper with his hand outstretched and emerged with the ball held high in it, signifying the catch. The batsman walked ruefully away in the direction of the pavilion, without waiting for the umpire to signify that he was out.

Commander Burt's opening sentence was:

"It didn't take you long to get a wicket, Jameson, did it! They were just settling down after lunch until you got here."

"Yes, sorry about that," replied Jameson jokingly, "but it was a bloody awful shot for a class batsman. He only seems able to get runs for Yorkshire. Bit of real pace and he's groping about like a blind man feeling for the heptagonal edge on a fifty pence piece!"

Commander Burt appeared to notice for the first time the difference in Peter Jameson's appearance and said:

"Good grief! I almost didn't recognise you. What's come over you? Are you going straight or something? If you'd grown a beard you'd have completed the disguise."

Jameson hoped he was not going to have this conversation each time he met an old acquaintance and half regretted the spur of the moment decision for the change but said:

"No, I just felt a bit fed up and thought a change of image might help."

"Well, I hope a change of image doesn't mean a change in you. After that last job you did for us you've got a reputation in the department as our most professional amateur. Which is why I've asked you back awhile..."

"Yes," interjected Jameson. "I thought it wasn't just to watch a Test Match – although I sure do appreciate the thought."

He let his mind wander back nine months or so, to when he had first been ushered into the presence of Britain's chief of security; he could not have imagined at the time that they would one day spend the afternoon at a cricket match enjoying this kind of relaxed banter.

The Commander was talking and this brought his mind back.

"As you know, we're concerned, as everyone is, about the recent spate of bombings. Although our bomb squad is doing a really first rate job, when we started to dig beneath the surface a little we found that, as is not unusual in our job, things weren't quite what they seemed."

"You mean," asked Peter, "it's not solely the IRA?"

"What I mean is, we don't think it is the usual partisan work of the IRA but we haven't reliable sources for finding out. We think they could be receiving organised assistance. Does that give you a clue why you're here?"

Jameson did not respond immediately.

Watching a peaceful cricket match it seemed inconceivable that the sixty year old security chief, Commander Burt, hiding under the guise of Head of Special Branch, and the man half his age who had been pressed (reluctantly) into government field service for less than a couple of years, could be discussing what was almost certainly the biggest single internal situation facing the government of the day. Applause rang round Lord's as England's new batsman, a young left-hander, smacked an overpitched delivery for four runs past cover point, and while the ball was retrieved Jameson said:

"I suppose anyone can pick up the phone and ring *The Daily Express*, put on an Irish accent and say, 'There's a bomb at Bond Street Underground Station, it has been planted by the provisional IRA'?"

"Precisely," replied the Commander. "But there's more to it than that. When this awful bomb business began it was carried out by fanatical lower ranks of the various Irish, and Irish sympathising, extremist organisations. But we've reason to believe others have entered the arena. People who make explosives, guns, military equipment, both in former communist countries and even in the USA. Yes, that is our whisper. America! And that came from an Allan Dallas source! You know you can only sell more bullets when the ones you've previously sold have been used."

"Yes, I appreciate that."

The Commander continued, barely noticing the interruption.

"Living in London you cannot have failed to have seen scattered over the capital, those derelict creatures we loosely call winos."

"Indeed. Usually sitting down in small groups in places like Lincoln's Inn Fields near the Law society, and under Waterloo bridge, or in Paddington. The ones who sleep in cardboard boxes. In fact the cardboard box brigade sleep anywhere. I had one of them lurch up to me only yesterday, with a bottle of cider sticking out of his overcoat pocket and his breath reeking of meths, asking me if I'd give him 10p for a cup of tea. When

I told him to shove off, he started shouting and screaming at me. It was quite funny really because a legal-looking guy came over and bashed him over the head with his umbrella and the wino ran off. Unfortunately, it bent the umbrella into a bow shape. I didn't quite know what to do so I took my benefactor for a drink. It was only then that I found out my legal friend had just passed his finals in the solicitors exams and had been heavily celebrating with his office colleagues and could hardly stand up himself. The umbrella had only been presented to him that day!"

"Looking at the weather we seem to be getting now, he shouldn't miss it," remarked the Commander with typical Burtian turn of phrase. He went on: "Can you cast your mind back some months to the two bomb blasts in London, one in Connaught Square and one thrown into the Plaza Restaurant in Covent Garden opposite the Opera House?"

"Well, I only heard sketchy reports about it, because of course I was at the training school, and as you may or may not know, you don't get very much time for relaxation," said Jameson artfully.

"Well, the one in Connaught Square went off prematurely killing the person who was pushing the bomb, a home-made job in a satchel, into place under a parked car. His death almost certainly saved the life of a woman passer-by, as he took the full blast and she only suffered some superficial cuts and nasty bruises. Nevertheless, pretty unpleasant for her."

Jameson nodded agreement.

"The bomb at the Plaza was a different story, however, eighteen people seriously injured including the bomber. The restaurant was packed with the after-theatre supper crowd. It couldn't have come at a worse time, for them, hell of a mess it made of the place, two people are still on the critical list and a third lost an eye from the flying glass. But a significant clue was found."

"Which was?" asked Jameson.

"Although the provisional IRA immediately claimed responsibility for both the outrages, we don't think they carried them out. In fact, both bombs were planted by these alcoholics we've just been talking about."

"And what does that mean?"

Commander Burt frowned at the interruption and continued.

"We know that the creature who threw the bomb into the Plaza was so out of his mind he couldn't have known what he was doing. An eye witness who was sitting in the window of the restaurant said that the man stood outside the entrance urinating into the gutter, swinging the satchel, his eyes were blurred and crazed. He was shouting or singing, you know the way these people do when they're 'full', when suddenly he swung the satchel through the air into the doorway of the restaurant. It went off on impact."

"What happened to the wino?"

"Ah, I was coming to that," replied Commander Burt. "This'll appeal to you. The blast blew the whole of his under carriage away. The ambulance men found him still holding his genitals in his hand, lying in the gutter, in his own urine."

Peter shuddered at the prospect. "It killed him of course?"

"No, not immediately. Fortunately for us we managed to keep him alive for two days, we wanted some info from him and he gave us what we wanted."

"What did he say?"

"He had no political opinions at all and was in fact Scottish. He'd been wandering the streets of London for the past two years. Just scrounging, begging, and sleeping rough."

The Commander began searching his pockets methodically for his pipe, and Peter Jameson let his mind run over this new twist to the bombing campaign in London and the home counties. It hadn't occurred to him before that forces other than those directly concerned in the problems of Ireland could be involved. But it began to become abundantly clear to him that, even leaving aside armaments, everything destroyed had to be replaced. An opening for the men with the suits. Buildings, cars, buses, shops; he began to see what the Commander was driving at, and asked:

"What exactly did you get out of this man then?"

"That he'd been given the satchel by a character who'd been sitting with them for several days and had been buying them booze. He'd been told the satchel contained fireworks and that the restaurateur wanted to claim loss of business from his insurance company. You know these people will believe anything."

"Some fireworks. How much did he get for that prank?" asked Jameson.

"Just five pounds," was the reply, "and he was to get another five when the job was done."

"Not exactly union rates was it, guv? OK, back to me," said Jameson, "where do I come into this business?"

"Investigative journalism for you boy – your radio skills!" said Commander Burt. "Your cover is that you are researching the background, the stories behind the bombings: poverty, broken homes, old hatreds and so on. You dig and you'll find someone is making money out of it. Of course, it would be a dangerous enough job if that's all you were doing, without working for us. It fits with your radio job, and your cloak for us as journalistic supernumerary!"

"And what the heck does that mean?" Asked a playful Jameson with a suggestion of a smile about his lips.

"It means nobody in Whitehall knows what you are doing, or why you're doing it should they ask," replied Burt seriously, "and it makes you the perfect candidate for this job!"

Jameson's lips switched into a full smile as he said irreverently, "It also makes 'em shit a brick if they think they are being looked at by the press. What have I got to go on, and how do you want me to work?" asked Jameson.

"Well, you can start off by picking up a woman. Yes, I thought this would stimulate your interest a little," said the Commander, as Peter shot him a swift surprised glance. "At a nightclub we know about."

"Man wasn't intended to sweat it all out under the armpits," said Jameson impudently, "Tell me more, how can I sacrifice myself for the cause? What sort of a girl?"

"A good-looking young lady who we think is Czechoslovakian."

"So you think there is communist involvement?"

"Believe me, Jameson. Communism has not died – it's just smouldering!" Burt said. "So, maybe. Could be, if only for commercial reasons, they're pretty broke! I've had men keeping watch on the areas where these winos are known to congregate and yesterday our vigilance was rewarded. A man answering the description given to us was seen sitting with a bunch of five of them on a circular seat outside the electricity board in Edgware Road."

"I know the one, it used to have a tree in the middle, but it now houses Safeway's bottle banks."

The Commander continued, "Right! We naturally had the man followed and he went to a flat just off the Bayswater Road, in Queensway."

"Hardly the address of a down-and-out," said Jameson.

"It had one of those security locks on the door so we couldn't see who answered it, he was admitted automatically after pressing the buzzer. However, the name below the buzzer was Anna Dubric – it's foreign, Eastern bloc. We've found out that she works at the Fanlight Club as a hostess." The Commander fished into his inside pocket and extracted a beige envelope, from this he withdrew a photograph. "I had one of our WPCs pose as a photographer there and she took this last night." He handed Jameson the envelope.

The girl was good looking in a rather Marilyn Monroe-ish sort of way. Good shoulders, full busted, blonde hair and large eyes were the immediate things which struck Peter Jameson as he said:

"Photographs can be very deceptive, especially ones taken with a flash."

"Oh," said Commander Burt, "she's a looker alright. She charges twenty quid minimum just to sit and talk to you and'll only drink champagne at Lord knows what a bottle."

"Good job I'm on expenses," chuckled Jameson. "I don't think I'll mind too much. I can see it's one of those 'tired businessman' places! Sounds just my thing, sir."

The players were trooping off the cricket field for the tea interval and Commander Burt said:

"Come on, I'll buy you that tea I promised."

During tea Commander Burt briefed Jameson. There was a singer pianist at the Fanlight Club named Mike who would be the go-between for the introduction to Anna. Jameson was ostensibly going to see Mike or rather to hear him with a view to his being used on the fortnightly, two-hour 'Peter Jameson Show'. This was bound to ensure the entertainer's keen cooperation. Jameson had been working as a radio DJ when recruited by Special Branch for one specific job involving radio, and, at Burt's insistence, he had retained his job with the BBC after the assignment's successful conclusion. Peter Jameson could not help thinking to himself that the old Commander did not miss a trick when it came to planning.

"Won't this Mike object to being cast in the role of a pimp?" he asked Commander Burt.

"Not at all, he's used to it and besides, he thinks he's the one being done a favour. You won't find it difficult to fit him into your radio show."

"You mean I've actually got to use him? Suppose he's no good?"

"Oh, he's good all right. You'll see. I heard him last night when I fixed all this up."

"You mean you went yourself. I'd have thought you'd have an underling on such an assignment," said Jameson.

"Aha," chuckled the Chief of Special Branch, "and so I would normally, but every now and again I have my little perks."

So his chief was human after all.

"Ask him to sing you 'Tears of a Child'," went on Commander Burt. "If you like it, you might even help him with it. He wrote it himself, sounds good, I think he's got talent."

*

It was a little after nine when Peter Jameson left the comfortable Knightsbridge flat deciding to have a drink before going on to the Fanlight Club. He chose a local pub, The Grenadier; set in a quiet mews near Hyde Park, the pub was supposed to be haunted by the ghost of a Grenadier Guards Officer, the walls of the place oozed a quiet history that appealed to Jameson.

The bar, split into pigeon holes by head high dividers, was very crowded so Jameson carried his beer to join the throng of people who'd spilled on to the terrace outside the pub. He was deep in thought when he received a violent knock from behind, jolting his elbow and sending the remainder of his beer over the lapel of his smart new designer suit. Jameson did not know it, but fate had just taken a hand.

"I'm terribly sorry, sunshine," a slightly slurred voice said, "caught my foot on the damned doorstep."

Jameson looked round aggrievedly at the cause of his misfortune and saw a tall lean man of around fifty, with strong features. He was smiling now, apologetically, but he was an aggressive-looking person and to Jameson he looked every inch the ruthless managing director of a company with a touch of no-nonsense policy.

"Can't be helped," said Jameson, "I should think that's how Mr Watney made most of his money, on beer spilt, certainly not on beer drunk. You need to drink ten pints of the stuff to even feel human these days." He began wiping his lapel, deciding the only thing for him to do was to make light of the accident.

"Well, let me get you another one, that's the least I can do."

"Thanks. I think I'll try the lager this time."

The man returned shortly with the beer and looked critically at Peter Jameson's lapel.

"Oh, that's going to be alright, could do with a clean anyway," he extended his hand. "The name's Mark Coggin. I was going to have a couple here and then on to my club. Care to join me?"

Peter Jameson gave his name to Coggin and then replied:

"Strangely enough that's exactly what I was going to do. I'm going to the Fanlight Club."

"What a bloody coincidence. That's my club. Been a member there for years." He leaned towards Jameson conspiratorially. "You won't have to pay if you go with me," he said.

"OK, then," said Jameson and, draining his drink, "let's grab a cab."

He thought, what a stroke of luck for him. What could be more natural than for him to arrive at the club in the company of a well-known member. They fell into step together and walked from the mews into Belgrave Square where they hailed a passing taxi.

Chapter 3
Anna

Anna Dubric had to concentrate hard in order to gaze steadily at Peter Jameson. After all she had had the best part of three bottles of Heidsack, and although they'd danced frequently in between the striptease acts which were a feature of the Fanlight Club the champagne was taking some effect. Peter Jameson, however, was feeling quite clear-headed. After the initial two glasses of bubbly drink, which were mandatory for all customers entertaining hostesses, he'd switched to Scotch and Coke and added lots of ice.

She shook his hand and, in a voice which had thickened over the past three hours, said:

"Will you be taking me home, darling? We close in about twenty minutes."

Before he could reply Mike the singer/pianist came over and joined them. After excusing himself for any interference, he said to Peter Jameson:

"Well, what do you think of the place?"

"If you really want to know what I think Mike, I think it's an expensive businessman's clip joint–"

"A cathouse, I call it," put in Mike grinning.

"–but it's quite well done. And furthermore, out of about fifteen hostesses working here, I've just been propositioned by the best-looking one."

If he expected Anna to be shocked he was disappointed. Her Czechoslovakian accent was appreciably more noticeable than it had been when Mike had first introduced them, and she merely said: "I couldn't agree more. Place is full of creeps. Mike will tell you I only sleep with people I like and I only get drunk with people I like."

At that she walked across the tiny dance floor, weaving in between the few remaining couples keeping up the pretence of dancing in the darkened atmosphere of the club.

"Don't blow it man," said Mike. "It's true what she says. Any of the other girls will go with anyone with money, but not Anna, she's very choosy. It's caused trouble here before, her being so choosy. Anyway, how do you like my act?"

"It's fine," replied Jameson. "But have you got any original material?"

"Sure, let me give you 'Tears of a Child'."

He went back to the tiny bandstand as Anna returned. After a brief word with the other musicians he began to play the piano and sang the words:

"Hello little girl, why are you crying..."

When he'd finished Anna said:

"That's beautiful. I don't think I've heard such a lovely song in ages."

"Yes, I like it too," replied Jameson, "and if you listen to my next show on Radio 1 you'll hear him sing it with full backing and an arrangement by Sly Singh, that'll make it sound ten times better."

A tall black woman who'd been dancing with Mark Coggin came over to Anna and whispered in her ear. She didn't whisper very softly as Jameson heard her say:

"Mark's drunk, but he's asked me to go on the Czechoslovakian arms run next time it goes. It sounds exciting. Is he really in that business, Anna? You know him."

He didn't hear Anna's reply as she turned her head away from his direction. He did notice, however, that Mark Coggin was settling the bill in dollar notes, a fact which struck him as decidedly odd. What he'd just overheard now added to his belief in the part luck can play in events, good or bad. Now his chance meeting with Mark Coggin was beginning to appear as if it had been ordained from above! This angular middle-aged playboy, who'd spilt inferior beer over his beautiful new designer suit in the earlier encounter, was now shaping up as a principal player in an illegal international arms trade. What further secrets might be wormed out in Anna's boudoir that night if he played his cards right? The black girl left after completion of their whispered conversation, and Anna interrupted Peter Jameson's reverie by pushing up close to him and whispering:

"You didn't answer me when I asked you if you would come home with me."

He forced himself not to sound too eager, sensing she was not the sort of girl to be impressed by such an attitude.

"Convince me," he said.

Unseen she rubbed her hand under the table across the top of his thigh, gently, and brushed her lips against his cheek.

"I promise you I'm very good if I like someone," she whispered seductively.

"I'm convinced," he whispered back in reply and they left the club some fifteen minutes later.

It had been dark at the club and it had not been very easy to assess the truth of Anna's good looks, although she was the sort of girl any man would not be ashamed to be seen with. Aged between twenty-five and thirty, her blonde hair, which she had worn up at the club, had now been let down and hung below her shoulders. Jameson noted that she had one of the largest bosoms he had ever seen. She smiled at him and walked through the door of her sitting room, where she had left him to make drinks, into her bedroom where she'd changed out of her evening dress. She now wore nothing except a lace gown which she had left partially open. She stood swaying slightly and as her eyes followed his as they travelled swiftly over her body, she said in a mocking voice:

"Are they too big for you?"

"I don't think so," he said and moved towards her.

She placed the forefinger of her right hand on his lips and said:

"Let's have a drink first eager beaver and a cigarette and a chat and then I will show you my bedroom."

He handed her a glass and as they sat down he aimed the question at her.

"You know most of the regulars at the club, Anna, what does Mark Coggin do for a living?"

At the mention of Coggin's name her eyes hardened.

"It's not a secret really, although he doesn't advertise the fact unless he's drunk. He's an arms dealer! But I thought you knew him?"

"No, not that well," he said and changed the subject.

He awoke the next morning with a splitting headache, but in splendid surroundings for such a malaise. Anna had been as good as she had said she would be and he let his eye run around the room to her dressing table where stood a three-quarters empty bottle of Bells whisky. He looked around him at the bed in which he was lying – a large French bed with crisp white sheets and a continental quilt; then to the floor where lay empty glasses. Yes, every picture tells a story, he thought to himself. Anna was not with him but he could hear her voice outside the door. He got up and crossed silently to place his ear to the bedroom door. She was talking on the telephone.

"But I thought he was a friend of yours, he came with you... What... How... I'll try... Wait... I think he's woken up, the snoring has stopped... alright, I said I'll try..."

He opened the door just as she was about to.

"Morning," he said, stifling a pretended yawn with his hand.

"Did you sleep well?" she asked.

"Not as well as I'm going to! Come here," he grabbed her and pulled her almost violently on to the bed. "Mornings are to be enjoyed not wasted."

She did not protest.

*

"Why did you ask me about Mark Coggin?" She asked him much later.

He decided to stay as close to fact as he could.

"No special reason except I bumped into him by accident in a pub and I was curious. I thought you might know something about him?"

He'd deftly turned the conversation so that he was the questioner without it appearing so. Now she had to answer his question. She did so by saying, "Peter, you be very careful with Mark Coggin, he's a very dangerous man. He scares me. He knows some very strange people, and that's all I can tell you."

Jameson decided it was time to go. Anna had provided him with the most interesting development – Coggin was an arms dealer and Jameson was there to investigate unusual explosions with a Fanlight Club connection! It would seem a good idea to find out more about Mr Coggin. He was sure that it had been he she was talking to on the phone when he'd woken, and that Coggin had been asking her questions about him. Why? Was it possible they were on to him? He walked across Hyde Park to his home, deep in thought, and after much deliberation came to the conclusion that however suspicious the circumstances might seem to him, his accidental meeting with Mark Coggin had been just that, an accidental meeting. Or had it?

He phoned Commander Burt as soon as he reached his home.

"I'd like to arrange for Mark Coggin's telephone to be temporarily bugged," he said as he explained what had happened, over the Commander's scrambled telephone line.

Chapter 4

Fears Unjustified

The first break came three days later. Peter Jameson had just finished reading the two minute news at the BBC when the newly promoted plain-clothed assistant to Commander Burt, Inspector Fisher, appeared in the engineer's box outside the 'on-air live' studio. The news had been sensationally bad – three bombings in London and one in Manchester. The Manchester bombing in the centre of the Piccadilly shopping area had claimed seventeen lives; two of the London ones had been defused and the third had killed a leading Labour Government politician as he'd placed the key to his car in the ignition. Belfast was in the middle of a riot which had still to be brought under control.

Jameson threw off his headphones in disgust at the end of the newscast. He was forced to keep his voice calm and impartial whilst 'on-air' but he could not prevent giving vent to his feelings privately. He went out of the studio to greet Fisher. It was the last newscast on his rota and he'd now finished for ten days. Inspector Fisher had changed almost beyond recognition since Jameson had first known him. Gone were the shabby raincoat and trilby hat. He'd grown a droopy moustache and added a full beard. He looked more like a dated hippie in his denim trousers and waistcoat, his dress for Broadcasting House.

After they were alone he said:

"We've had our first positive major lead."

It transpired that installing the tiny transmitter in Mark Coggin's Mayfair offices had presented no problems to Q Department. It was not, however, so easy to monitor. Later Jameson was to gather covert information more effectively. They had discovered that Coggin dealt legitimately in arms, but to make things more difficult, he had a habit of moving from office to office, making and receiving telephone calls. Q Department had hours of tape through which they had systematically sifted discovering that most of it was worthless. Some names would be discreetly checked out over the course of the next few days. However, the break which had brought Fisher hurrying over to Broadcasting House was the information that Mark Coggin would be travelling north by train to meet a man from America, referred mysteriously to as HH, but the word 'Provos' had been used in conversation. He was expected at Yeadon Airport in Yorkshire and would be travelling in his private jet. The instruction from the department was that Fisher and Jameson would be travelling to Yorkshire by train that afternoon.

*

Inspector Fisher paid off the taxi at Kings Cross main line train station and he and Jameson headed towards the re-vamped entrance. They stopped at the Smiths bookstall, Fisher examining the 'girlie' magazines while Jameson thumbed through the novels.

"Why hello, sunshine," a voice said in his ear. "What are you doing here?"

Jameson started, the voice belonged to Mark Coggin. Fisher very quickly moved to the edge of the bookstall, caught the eye of the girl behind the counter and paid her for the magazine he had in his hand. Keeping his back to Coggin and Jameson, he melted into the throng of people all heading in the direction of the trains travelling towards the north.

Jameson turned towards the direction of the voice and said:

"Why, Mark Coggin! I don't believe it," and jokingly, "you're a long way from the Fanlight Club. You'll see I'm wearing a raincoat this time in case you decide to pour beer over me!"

Coggin smiled. "Ah, the Fanlight Club, that's pleasure, sunshine, this is business."

Before anything more could be said the station public address system crackled into life and a muffled female voice in somnolent tones announced barely distinguishably that "the train now standing at platform seven is the express train to Leeds, stopping at Watford Junction, Grantham, Bradford and Leeds."

"That's me," said Jameson.

"And me," replied Coggin. "What're you going there for?"

"Oh, I'm doing a documentary for the BBC," lied Peter "You know, background behind the Irish problems, the bombings and all that. The production is at their Leeds studios."

"Well," said Coggin "we may as well pass four hours together. I'm on my way to meet a business colleague coming in from the States."

"The States. Funny place to come in."

"Private jet. That's why the Yanks are up and we're down. They don't mess about. Who wants to circle Heathrow for an hour, and spend another in customs, when you can land straight away at Yeadon with the minimum of formalities."

They fell into step together in the direction of Platform 7.

"I'm afraid the Beeb don't run to providing us with first class tickets," said Jameson, "but I'll sit with you until the ticket inspector kicks me out."

"Don't worry, sunshine," replied Coggin "when he does we'll go and stand at the bar."

Peter Jameson had already noticed as they'd walked along the platform in the direction of the first class carriage, Inspector Fisher, two carriages down, slumped in a corner seat, his face partially hidden by his hastily purchased magazine. Poor old

Fisher he thought, the magazine he was stuck with was *Teen Scene*.

"There's something odd about you, Peter," said Coggin probingly, "you don't seem the typical broadcasting type to me, but then I know you are, because I hear you everywhere I go and you keep popping up every now and again like a weed on TV. Although just lately not quite as much."

"Well, I've been involved in research for this documentary. But I'm not from a traditional broadcasting background," said Peter. "Originally I was the typical, keen,

up-and-coming business lad, passed all my marketing exams and all that. I found my openings, used them and got pretty high up the ladder. I built up a company, together with others of course, and then one day a very big company took our company over. I was very young and the new company had their own marketing director. I was given the push and exactly one grand. I was naturally very disappointed so I decided I'd drop out of business. Went away for a while."

Mark Coggin listened attentively.

Jameson thought, 'I must be giving him what he wants to hear,' as he could see the interest in Mark Coggin's eyes. He went on:

"When I came back the 'pirate' radio stations were just beginning. I joined one. At first I was terrible, but then we all were. But I practiced and concentrated and gradually I got good at the job. And here I am!"

"Just the stuff Great Britain is made of," chuckled Coggin. "I'll tell you my story some day when you know me better."

"Why not now?"

"Nah – take too long, and besides," he looked at his watch "nearly at Watford Junction. Time to go for a drink, what do you say?"

Jameson knew he'd get no further so gave up, but he'd felt he was just beginning to get inside Mark Coggin. Perhaps that should be the approach to cultivate the man, you invite a line by giving a line! Well, there were another three hours to go.

"Why not?" he replied.   "Nothing like a drink to while away the time."

Chapter 4

Q'd in to HH

The train rattled and clunked its way over the junction points on the outskirts of Watford as Jameson followed Mark Coggin along the corridor of the train. The buffet bar, as usual, was in the last carriage of the train which meant a journey for them of almost the entire train's length. They passed a 'Toilet Vacant' sign and Jameson tapped Coggin on the shoulder.

"We'll have earned that drink by the time we get there," he said and as Coggin nodded, added, "it's either the cold weather or the shaking of this train but I've got to go," and he continued as he placed his hand on the door handle. "Tell you what, I'll join you at the bar. Mine's a G & T."

After he'd closed and locked the door he produced a BBC business card from his waistcoat pocket and scribbled on its back the words, 'bring a Q9 to me in the bar – urgent!'

Having done this he made use of the facilities although the train had now come to a halt at the station. Passengers were alighting and boarding the train, doors were slamming everywhere and whistles blowing as Jameson reached the compartment in which Inspector Fisher sat. The compartment door was halfway open and Peter slipped the business card into Fisher's hand, and continued on his way to the buffet bar as the train jolted into motion and began to pick up speed. Mark Coggin was already in flippant conversation with a dark, heavily made-up girl, when he arrived. Jameson guessed, rightly as it turned out, that she was a demonstrator. He had to hand it to Coggin, he was a smooth, fast operator.

"Ah, there you are, sunshine," said Coggin loudly above the increasing clatter of the train. "Come and meet Maria." He effected the introductions and said to her: "Only trouble with Peter here is he's got a weak bladder that's why he keeps getting... ha-ha," and to Peter "I'm afraid she's drinking your drink. Never mind we'll all have another. Three more large ones," he called across to the barman.

"Maria demonstrates Russian perfumes," continued Coggin solemnly to Jameson, "and did you know the Russians are the largest producers of perfume in the world!"

"Geewhizz," said Jameson feigning incredulity. "I knew the Russians were stinkers and this kinda proves it!"

The girl was an unexpected complication for Jameson. The Q9 that he'd asked Fisher to bring to him was the department's 'knock-out' pill. It had been specially developed by the department and was no ordinary sleep inducer. To begin with it was half the size of an aspirin, white in colour, and dissolved instantly upon immersion in liquid with merely the faintest fizz. Ideal for use with gin and tonic, Jameson had been told by the head of Q Department. It took exactly ten minutes to take effect, kept the subject 'out like a light' for a further thirty minutes, and it took another ten minutes for them to come round. Its unique property, however, was that, from beginning to end, the subject would have no idea that he or she had been drugged.

Inspector Fisher approached and Jameson furiously scratched his cheek with his left index and forefinger splayed upwards, hoping that Fisher would get the message. Two Q9s were now needed. The train lurched and as Fisher bumped briefly against him Jameson felt Fisher's hand go in and out of his right hand pocket. Fisher bought some cigarettes and a packet of crisps, muttered his thanks to the bartender who returned to his glass polishing and left the buffet car without a glance in Jameson's direction.

Cautiously Jameson felt in his pocket, and was relieved to find that Fisher had taken no chances, four little Q9s were lodged in the corner of his pocket.

In other circumstances Peter Jameson would have been happy with the prospect of chatting to Maria, as she was a dark-haired 'looker' with an effervescent personality, for the rest of the journey. But he knew that what he wanted was to see the contents of Mark Coggin's briefcase, which was on the floor at Coggin's feet. As the train sped on he made his opening move in that direction.

"Why don't we take some drinks with us and go back to our compartment?" he asked. "After all we've got more than two hours before we hit Bradford and we might as well get drunk in comfort."

"Good idea, sunshine," said Coggin. "Maria can demonstrate to us how she sells that Russian perfume. It must be very hard when you're competing with the established French market."

She smiled and said, "On the contrary Mark. As the Russians produce more perfume than any other country in the world you just use more of it!"

"Sounds like something out of your sales manual," replied Coggin.

Jameson got up, and in three steps crossed the swaying buffet car to the bar. He ordered eight miniature gins (eight doubles should be enough he thought), and two cans of tonic.

"Come on," he said after he'd made the purchase, "lets go!"

It was not difficult once they'd returned to their first class compartment, for Jameson to give both of them a Q9 and, exactly to schedule, within the ten minutes they began to get sleepy. Coggin tried to fight it but the girl just said:

"The trains swaying so much that I think I'll put my feet up and have a little nap. I'm not sure if I'm tiddly or tired, or tired or tiddly," she giggled.

But before she could literally put her feet up the drug overcame her and she slumped in the corner.

Coggin's eyes were closing but Jameson waited until Coggin had become totally immobile. Then swiftly he reached down and pulled Coggin by his heels and laid him along the seat in the railway compartment. That way it would appear as though just another innocent traveller had fallen asleep on the train. Then he turned his attention to the girl. As he picked her up by the heels he gasped. Her skirt had fallen upwards to reveal the fact that she wore no underwear, only a complicated pair of crotchless tights. The hair from her pubis staring starkly at Peter Jameson was light brown, in sharp contrast to the raven colour crowning her head. Just goes to show, he thought to himself, as he laid her gently across the seat, travelling girls should be prepared for every eventuality! At least she had a smile on her face! The carriage door slid open and Inspector Fisher appeared.

"I've been hanging about outside here for nearly a quarter of an hour," he exclaimed.

"Right, let's move fast," said Peter Jameson. "Give me your kit and take your eyes off that woman. She's scenery!"

He took from Fisher the tiny burglary kit proffered and before picking up Mark Coggin's briefcase, drew on the thin surgeon-like rubber gloves. There would be no fingerprints here. Fisher had done likewise. Next he inserted a tiny file into the delicate mechanism of the combination lock on the briefcase and after a few exploratory probes, the lock sprang back.

"How's that for speed," he said to Fisher.

"Marvellous," replied Fisher sardonically and handed Jameson an instrument which looked like an ordinary pencil torch. It was, however, rather special. It could be used for three purposes: explosive detection, electronic detection (bugs) and as an ordinary torch.

"We'd look a right couple of Charlies if that briefcase blew us all out of the train," he said pointedly.

Jameson ran the delicate instrument over the case. It bleeped once as it passed over a pair of neatly folded grey socks. Gingerly he lifted them out and there, underneath, was a Beretta automatic pistol. Carefully he removed it and the bleeping ceased. Delicately he drew back the firing hammer and removed the firing pin. Swiftly they examined the remainder of the briefcase's contents.

There was an interesting assortment of papers and as Fisher produced a tiny Minox camera and began photographing the papers, Peter Jameson thumbed through the leather-bound address book he'd found in the case.

The names, mostly, meant nothing to him, but some of them had a familiar ring to them. Lord Gilhauley was a prominent Northern Irish Peer and industrialist, as was Lord Lander. He'd been security adviser to the governing administration. He handed the book to Fisher.

"You'd better get this on film," he said, and turned his attention to a leather-bound ring file which nestled neatly in what appeared to be a specially constructed compartment in the case. As he turned the pages of this book the expression on his face changed from astonishment to bewilderment and finally amazement, as the full realisation struck him.

"Hey, Fish," he called across to Fisher who was perched in the furthermost corner of the carriage, his tiny camera clicking furiously, "take a look at this," and as he handed it to the Inspector he said, "we've got a blackmail document here!"

Fisher let out a low whistle as he too glanced through its contents.

"But it seems to be incomplete. Wait, I've got it. These are the additions to a main list." He held four frames of transparent film to the light, which were part of a sheaf of films he had found at the rear of the book. "Just look at this, this stuff's dynamite."

Jameson peered at the film. It was a revolting spectacle, involving a naked woman and man, a dog, and a young girl and boy watching. A tiny reference had been scratched in the bottom left hand corner of the negative. He took the leather-bound book from Fisher and turned the pages to the reference;

there he found the appropriate entry, it read: 'Mrs Jane Lumley aged thirty-nine. Daughter of Sir Charles and Lady Bradfield. Employed as first assistant to Mr Nigel Harrington Treasury Department, see ref H.3.' It read: 'Mr Nigel Harrington aged forty-three. Son of the late Reverend Thomas Harrington, second Junior Assistant, Treasury Department, see L.9.'

"Now I get the operation, blackmail," he said. "Those people in this book," he patted the leather bound ring file, "are new business and that could be one of the reasons why this mysterious HH is arriving at Yeadon this evening in the private jet."

Inspector Fisher consulted his watch.

"We've got about ten minutes before those two," he nodded towards the incumbent Coggin and the girl, "start to come round."

As they replaced the contents of the briefcase Peter Jameson's thoughts raced at the speed of the express train in which he was travelling. From what he'd seen, the papers they were so carefully replacing were evidence of nothing less than treason. But they needed a lot more information. He said to Fisher:

"I think we are going to have to take a chance. What do you say we plant a QBX?"

This was one of the department's most sophisticated transmitters. Tiny in size, no larger than a boiled sweet, non-detectable electronically and once its battery expired, it would self-destruct. Its disadvantages were that it had a range of only thirty yards and a battery life of twenty hours. Inspector Fisher broke the seal of the transmitter and slipped the tiny instrument into Mark Coggin's top pocket, the receiver, which looked exactly like a deaf aid, he slipped into his own ear. In low tones the two men planned their operation. Inspector Fisher was to have the task of following Mark Coggin to Yeadon Airport and of monitoring the incoming talks between Coggin and HH, Peter Jameson would establish their base in a Bradford

Hotel, and contact London for the back-up they needed for this operation.

"Leave everything in your compartment when you get off the train in Bradford, Fish," Jameson said looking at his watch, "and I'll have it taken with my own stuff to the Royal, that's where I'll be. And now you'd better get the hell out of here, hadn't you? They'll be back in the land of the living, like any minute now!"

Inspector Fisher looked carefully round the compartment. He appeared slightly incongruous in his blue denim, in sharp contrast to the smart dress of the other three. But Fisher's trained eye was checking each detail systematically. Finally he seemed satisfied.

"Stick this in your case," he said handing Jameson the Minox; then he slid back the compartment door, and disappeared along the corridor of the speeding express train.

By the time Maria and Mark Coggin awoke, Peter Jameson had moved them into upright positions opposite one another in one corner of the compartment and he himself was feigning sleep in a third corner. It was the arrival of the ticket inspector, fortunately, which gave the air of a natural awakening, and the £5 note which Jameson gave him disappeared miraculously into his pocket without the formality of excess fare documentation.

Somehow, throughout the remainder of the journey to Bradford, Peter Jameson managed to avert his eyes from Mark Coggin's top pocket, he concentrated on the girl. He'd already established that she was booked into the Royal for two weeks, and he amused himself letting his mind run riot on how best to take advantage of his accidentally gained specialist knowledge of her. He smiled at Maria, but she had no means of knowing what was behind his smile.

Chapter 5
Meet HH

The distinctively marked executive jet aeroplane, the property of Henry Howerd, known to his immediate circle as HH, winged its way across the Atlantic Ocean at a steady 600mph. The aircraft had been arranged to accommodate the trappings of the very rich American entrepreneur even to the extent of the installation of the gold-plated bath in which he now reposed. His fetish for extreme cleanliness was well-known. Although considered an eccentric, and sometimes a recluse, this was a man of total dedication. He was tough and unyielding. Nobody worked for HH without having similar characteristics.

"Bring me a bathrobe, Hal, will yuh," he called out to the mountain of a man who served as a bodyguard.

Once out of his bath and huddled in his robe, HH examined the contents of one briefcase. It contained the equivalent of $2,000,000, equally divided into four currencies – dollars, sterling, Deutschmarks, and Belgian francs. The money had come to HH via his 'collectors'. This was an organised group of people who raised money from members of the American public who had been persuaded to part with cash to assist the cause of the IRA. Much of the money would find its way back to HH via his arms and explosives corporation – Friendship Manufacturing Factors and other companies. HH rustled through papers in his Irish briefcase, as he called it, for some time, checking records of recent dealings in the Irish Republic and Northern Ireland. He examined contracts obtained and contracts lost; at what price and to whom. He looked at payments made from his 'Slush Fund' and checked the recipients' names against contracts awarded, whether to his companies or to rival organisations. Those officials who accepted his bribes would be squeezed at a later stage as had already happened with some of their predecessors. There were prominent, and indeed eminent, names on file – Pension Fund managers, construction contractors, government officials – the Henry Howerd Organisation covered a very wide spectrum. But it was not these people HH currently probed. Somebody in his own organisation was fiddling him, cheating him out of vast sums of money. He consulted his watch before calling to his bodyguard who was sitting in the front section of the aircraft.

"Tell the pilot to file a flight plan for Shannon Airport, Hal," he said. "Yes, that's in Ireland. I have some business to attend to with a shit from the IRA."

"Sure thing HH," The man swivelled round in his seat. "Anything of interest to me?" he enquired. He enjoyed the strong arm functions he performed for his boss and he now sensed some action.

"Yes, I think you will earn yourself a maximum bonus during our short stay in Ireland. Someone in my organisation has been cheating me, and you know I don't like that. But... I have narrowed the contenders down to two people. Now you go give those flight instructions to the pilot and bring me back the radio phone. I will have the ultimate candidate singled out before we reach Ireland."

"Sure will, HH," Hal called out as he moved forward in the direction of the flight deck.

Immediately the radio phone arrived with its acoustic cowling to ensure privacy even from his own staff, HH made a series of telephone calls via satellite. Finally he cradled the phone and removed the cowling. He called his man over.

"OK Hal," he said, "I know who it is. It's a man named Connelly, and this is how we play it."

*

Inspector Fisher was having a hard time. He was crouched in the corner of a tiny closet no larger than a double bed at the end of the corridor of a hotel. The closet entrance was covered by a curtain.

He listened to the conversation of the two men who occupied the luxury suite at the other end of the corridor. So far they had said nothing of relevance and the small cassette recorder in Fisher's hand remained ready for use but switched to 'off'.

Disembarking from the London/Leeds Express at Bradford Station, Inspector Fisher had hurried ahead of Coggin to Yeadon Airport. Because of the special nature of his mission Fisher carried no official identification, but one telephone call to the special number he gave to the Security Official not only ensured his swift passage into the stark offices of Immigration, but gained him a look of profound respect from that official.

The private plane had already arrived and immigration had, in keeping with normal practice in the case of VIPs, appeared to afford it and its occupants minimum formalities. In reality, however, in response to Special Branch's request, the sharp-eyed customs officials who'd boarded the plane had given the aircraft and its occupants a very thorough check over. The aircraft with a crew of four was on lease from a Swiss company, Air Charter, to an American stock-dealing company with international conglomerates. There were four male passengers and one female. Brief informal questions from the immigration official who'd accompanied the two customs officers revealed a harmless enough picture. Penelope Armstrong was a plain but efficient-looking private secretary to Henry Howerd, whose passport showed his profession as a financier. He was accompanied by an accountant, a nervous little man who constantly adjusted his glasses and fiddled with his tie, and two hefty private bodyguards. They were all Americans and had flown from the States. The pilot had applied for his last flight plan from Chicago's O'Hare Field but had re-routed to refuel at Shannon Airport in Ireland.

"They're in the VIP lounge now," the official had told Fisher.

"How can I take a look at them without them seeing me?" Fisher had asked.

"Easy," had come the reply. "We've got a two-way window. It's not all moors and sheep in Yorkshire, you know."

Fisher smiled and followed the official into a conference room where the wide angle window gave a perfect view of the VIP lounge. His guide explained to him in his friendly Yorkshire accent, that when Yeadon Airport had been built it had been hoped that the airport would attract its share of international air traffic; a hope which so far remained a hope and the airport was losing money heavily. Fisher had a clear view of the party below. Henry Howerd was giving instructions to his secretary who was taking notes. Howerd looked a tycoon, you'd know this man had money and power at a glance. He had a strong slim face; dark, trimmed moustache; wore a medium grey business suit, and although the overcoat was draped carelessly over a chair (it was cashmere), he still wore his grey Homburg hat, and dark glasses. There were hard lines of ruthlessness etched into his face and Fisher adjudged him to be about fifty.

At that moment Coggin entered the lounge. The receiver in Fisher's ear crackled as he came into range. Now Fisher could clearly hear the voices. Henry Howerd had one of those deep bass voices which only Americans seem to possess. Coggin appeared to be familiar with all present although formal handshakes were made all round.

Business was not mentioned in the VIP lounge, nor was it during the twenty minute drive to Bradford's best hotel, and there was still nothing to record.

Fisher was beginning to feel a numbness creeping into his left leg, he shifted it and as he did so heard the American's deep voice say:

"Well, Coggin, you've eaten well, drunk well and talked well so now to business. I didn't set you up just so's you can screw every broad in London."

"I thought you'd never ask HH. We're doing very well in all departments." Fisher heard footsteps, and a snapping of clasps which he attributed to Coggin's briefcase being opened.

"I think you'll be pleased with that." There was a pause as the American examined the documents that had been discovered earlier, Fisher smiled, he knew its contents.

HH said: "You haven't made approaches to these yet?"

"No, of course not. Your instructions were no moves until you give the personal OK. There's a small problem though, the girl, Anna, is getting restless. She doesn't know why the girls need to get these sort of pictures but she's beginning to suspect it's some kind of extortion. A coloured girl recognised Lord Lander. I've handled it – told her I'd send her on a trip to Czechoslovakia, where it'll be arranged for her to disappear, but it started Anna thinking. She wants more money, and she wants us to fulfil our agreement to get her mother out of Czechoslovakia and over here."

"Can you replace her? Anna, I mean," the hard tones of the American reverberated in Fisher's ear.

"She knows too much to stay alive," was the reply from Mark Coggin.

"I'll arrange it then," said HH and went on, "look here, Coggin, nothing is going to interfere with my European operation and certainly not some dumb broad. I want my chain of power in the UK strengthened."

Fisher heard his fist bang the table.

"You know I can exert more power in the US than the President if I want to. They come to me for money for their stupid election campaigns – but they don't even know who I am. I'm just a name. I change my appearance when I feel like it and I can walk around unrecognised and yet, through my nominees, I'm the richest person in America. And that's how I want it in the UK. Do you think it's an accident that your pound drops and drops?" he asked. "It's not! I decided five years ago to take advantage of all your strikes to enhance my overseas banking profits. With the total inability of your workforce to harmonise with management, I use a tactic I developed through experienced gained with my own teamsters union in the United States: which was to strike and strike and strike. Strike at every opportunity for more money. And they did. The poor bastards only just realised they paid most of what they got back in taxes, so now they strike for a shorter working week and when they get it demand overtime. But what it was doing to the country was stripping it of its assets. And you know who is getting those assets?" he chuckled "Me. And some of the Arabs I can work terrorist and arms deals with. My banks operate in all currencies and countries and although they are under different banners, they all belong to me. So you see, when your treasury lets the pound slip three or four cents, I am delighted. My banks all over the world buy. They buy millions! And when it goes up again a few cents, they sell.

"I make millions. That's quite legit. But I don't want to gamble. So I manipulate the treasury. I know when to buy and when to sell. It's like having a crystal ball. But I want it watertight – want it strengthened – and that means every important official. That's why this stuff is good."

HH consulted his wristwatch. It was 9 p.m. He walked across the room to switch on the TV set.

"We should make this news bulletin, I fixed it on my way over here," he explained mildly to Coggin as the sound came on. The news theme faded and the newscaster's voice was mixed in with the headlines:

'Another killing in Ireland; the Government calls for greater worker cooperation with its fellow workers; and the Iron Lady rattles on.'

"Good evening. Just two hours ago a man named as William Connelly was shot dead in a gentlemen's lavatory at Shannon Airport. It is not yet known why Connelly was at Shannon Airport. The possibility has not been ruled out that he was there for a secret meeting with members of a US organisation funding the IRA. At the time, a Pan Am flight was on stopover from Chicago to London. The flight has been suspended and passengers are still being interviewed by the police. The Provisional IRA have already claimed that Connelly was suspected by British Security of being a top member of the IRA executive, an accusation they deny, and they claim Mr Connelly was murdered by British security forces in a show of strength against them. A substantial sum of foreign currency was found on Connelly's body and a senior detective said the matter was being treated as murder and investigated accordingly."

HH snapped the set off.

"Connelly tried to cheat me, Mark," and, "there are lessons to be learned," he said in soft tones, but his voice rose to its tough flinty level and he bared his teeth in a mirthless smile, saying:

"But nobody cheats HH. But nobody. He was a good man but too ambitious for his own good," he sighed. "A great shame to see a good man wasted."

Fisher could picture the mysterious Henry Howerd, if that was his real name, patting the documents Coggin had handed over. He could scarcely believe what he was hearing. It all seemed like a storyteller's fantasy. But the picture was revealing itself to him in dreadful detail. The blackmail evidence he'd seen pertaining to the two junior officials in the Treasury was only the tip of the iceberg, from what he could make out, more important officials were already under the control of this ruthless man. Fisher changed the tiny cassette, automatically slipping the recorded spool inside his denim waistcoat. What an explosion this was going to cause when Commander Burt listened to this evidence. It was beyond his comprehension as to what action Burt would be able to take. Who could he talk to? From the Inspector's privileged position of knowing the general outline of the plan by one man's organisation to take financial control of the United Kingdom, it appeared to him that the heart of the system had been compromised. Who was involved and who wasn't?

It seemed that HH had, through Coggin, treated the whole project as a gigantic sales campaign. But in this instance people were the product. Having found the product, explore for an opening, in this case a weakness. If the product did not possess a weakness by which they could be forced to comply with the marketing organisation, they created one. HH's organisation had even exploited the Irish situation and had almost certainly penetrated the various movements involved in that power struggle. After all, money and arms came from somewhere and it had never satisfactorily been explained where all the money came from.

*

The curtains behind Inspector Fisher's head parted and the brute-like figure of HH's bodyguard loomed in the opening. He surveyed the scene for a split second and then as Inspector Fisher's head began to turn towards him he wielded the loaded rubber cosh from behind his head with sickening force. It struck Inspector Fisher a terrible blow, crushing the sensitive side of the head between the ear and the temple. It killed him instantly and his body keeled over. The receiver fell from his ear and the cassette recorder dropped from his lifeless grasp.

The bodyguard surveyed the scene, this was not the first time he'd administered violent death. He could hear the conversation of his employer and Mark Coggin coming from the fallen miniature receiver. He stepped over the lifeless body and grasped it under the armpits, then after looking swiftly along the empty corridor he dragged the body towards the closed door behind which the two men, whose conversation

Inspector Fisher had given his life to overhear, were still talking.

"What the hell..." Said Coggin as he began taking in the sight of Fisher's lifeless body. "This isn't Chicago! You're in England. Who is he?"

The bodyguard ignored him and dragged the body past him into the room.

"Found him in the maid's closet at the end of this corridor, Ted," he said to HH. "Take a look at the equipment." He showed the receiver which had been in the policeman's ear, and the cassette recorder. Henry Howerd's face showed an emotion Coggin had never seen on it before: fear, but that fleeting chink in his armour quickly disappeared. The face became expressionless again.

"Don't use that name here!" He said tersely to the minder, and went on, "You must have been followed," he said to Coggin.

"Impossible!" exclaimed Coggin. "No way. I've never seen him... and that thing's still working so there must be a hidden bug. Who is he?"

He bent over the fallen Fisher. Blood was trickling from the deep wound on the side of his head and staining the thick pile carpet. An examination of the dead man's pockets proved fruitless.

"Did you expect a calling card, Coggin?" said HH. "Give Hal a hand with him. Get him up to Hal's room, he's staining my carpet."

Coggin looked briefly at the American. His will was like iron. He said nothing and, swallowing his pride, stooped down and picked the corpse up under the armpits.

"Come on, Hal," he said gruffly to the American bodyguard, and together they carried the body along the corridor, up the service stairs to the bodyguard's room.

Coggin closed the bedroom door, observing that it was a double room. He was sweating visibly from the exertion and removed his jacket. He still wore the large Homburg. He threw the jacket over the foot of the bed and then pulled the handkerchief from the top pocket to mop his brow. The tiny transmitter fell out of the pocket and rolled under his bed unnoticed. Fisher, even in death, had cheated them. By the morning the transmitter would just be the tiniest puff of dust and it was the transmitter which would have connected Fisher with Special Branch. This would have amounted to leaving a calling card.

The two men returned to the multi-millionaire's suite. He was seated upon the chintz couch examining Fisher's tiny receiver/recorder as the two men entered.

"It's stopped receiving which means the connection has been broken," he said. "But the transmitting bug has to be on you or in this room."

Coggin was searched thoroughly but to no avail. The matter remained a mystery.

"No matter, no matter, it's not important now," said HH impatiently.

"Leave us alone, Hal," he said. "Go join the others but stay close. Where are they?"

"Your secretary's in the bar with the book crook and Buzz's in the car. He digs himself in a Rolls Royce, even if it is rented."

"OK. OK. Take off."

"There can be only one explanation for that man's presence here," HH said to Coggin, "and it's got to be you. Somehow it looks as though the British have gotten on to you, but the question is how much do they know?"

There was a pause before Mark Coggin cleared his throat and said thoughtfully, "Supposing one of our victims has been doing some private investigations? Any one of a dozen people from a Cabinet minister to a junior assistant could have the resources, but I should think if it was an official investigation, there'd be more than one man and, if so, we'd have seen some action by now."

"You could be right," conceded HH. "You could just be right."

"If only Hal hadn't been so damned heavy-handed we'd soon have been able to find out," complained Mark Coggin.

There was silence for the best part of a moment as both men considered all the possibilities. HH broke the silence:

"We can't afford any chances. We'll have that body disposed of in a desolate spot on these Yorkshire Moors. With any luck it won't be discovered for a long time. Now I'll send the plane back without me on it early tomorrow, and then you and I will travel by train to Dover, take the boat to the continent and then you can slip into Eastern Europe through Vienna. I think you should be out of circulation for a while."

HH picked up the phone to contact his secretary and while he was waiting for her to be paged, said to Coggin, "I'm gonna send two of my men over here to oversee your operation, while you're out of sight. They'll keep contact with the girls – how many of them are there now?"

"Sixteen," came the reply.

"And they'll step up the bombings which they'll run from Berkeley Square. Our Irish contacts are getting a bit restless and so are the Russians."

He broke off and began issuing rapid instructions into the phone. He had no need to tell his secretary to take notes. She was far too efficient to enter a phone booth to talk to HH without a notepad in her possession.

The speed at which the man worked was a wonder to behold. In the space of less than ten minutes, all their arrangements had been made, including the disposal of the late Inspector Fisher. Almost as an afterthought, instructions were given for the acquisition of the London merchant bank, Grindlays. He replaced the telephone receiver in its ornate cradle and turned to Mark Coggin.

"Get hold of Lord Lander in the morning, will you Mark?" he said, "And tell him he's to be President. Moynahan's too Irish. You know this is my first bank in the UK and I want a good public figure fronting it. He can arrange the finance through the Swiss division of Leasebroking International. My secretary will take care of the Swiss end. There'll be a credit of £30,000,000 for transfer to Grindlays' London account."

In the plush surroundings of HH's Bradford Hotel suite the two men discussed their revised plans.

Mark Coggin's companies, Benson Consolidated, Benson Shipping and Benson Sales would continue to function as normal in his absence but the illegal aspects of the business, the shipping of arms and explosives on carefully planned routes from Czechoslovakia to Northern and the Republic of Ireland would be supervised by the two Americans. They were also specialists in extortion and blackmail having learned their trade at very young ages from the mobs in Chicago and Philadelphia. They would make contact with the small band of men Coggin had so successfully recruited to supplement the IRA bombing efforts in London and the provinces. And they would also keep the contact with Anna who controlled the sixteen or so high class call girls, specialising in compromising high ranking officials.

Anna was to be allowed to continue in her role for the time being but the blackmail evidence would be constantly up-dated. Coggin's absence would create no suspicion either in his legitimate or illegitimate organisations as it was not unusual for him to be abroad for short or, occasionally, long periods of time. Coggin on the other hand thought the situation being unfolded was distinctly dangerous for him. The arrival of his boss's two henchmen from America to literally take over the structure he had painstakingly built up set the scene for him. The man in the large hat now studying him and urbanely offering him a drink, he realised was totally ruthless. Had he not just witnessed more of the man's plans and ambitions, before the death of the unknown investigator, than was good for him? The unknown man's discovery, although fortunate for them both, had changed the whole concept of the UK operation. He, Coggin, was now under intense scrutiny and that made his recently gained knowledge very dangerous for Henry Howerd. Coggin had had no idea that this man had been using the blackmail evidence for a personal assault on sterling and that already these operations had drained the country's resources of millions and millions of pounds. And the stark fact was that he, Mark Coggin, was the one man who knew all this. He shivered inwardly and decided he'd have to watch himself very, very carefully. He needed some personal insurance otherwise he could see himself ending his days in the manner of the recently departed William Connelly.

Chapter 6

Further Developments

Peter Jameson lay drowsily in bed, his eyes flickering open and then closing. He was in Maria's bed in Maria's room and it was just dawn as he lay by her side sleeping the sleep of exhaustion. Their clothes lay scattered in a trail from the table where they'd sat drinking the champagne he'd bought with him, to bed, where Maria's black bra was hanging, swinging from the knob of the headboard of the old-fashioned bed. It was the last garment he'd removed before she had turned out the light, which he had promptly turned on again, saying softly, "Hey, come on. I like to see where I'm going," and surveying her, said emphatically, "you've got nothing to be ashamed of Maria."

At this her self-consciousness had melted away and they'd enjoyed a night of natural bliss.

With an effort Jameson dragged himself from the bed, noting the dark shadows beneath the eyes of the sleeping Maria. His eyes moved downward to her shoulders and bosom as she lay on her side, half uncovered. Her breasts were large, rounded and full with one noticeably larger than its companion. They made an exciting picture lifted and angled against the snowy whiteness of the sheet covering the mattress. Jameson crept back into the bed beside her. With his hands he gently fondled her, cupping her breasts, and with his fingers he explored the areolae surrounding the sensitive area of the nipples. She sniffed and snuggled her back into his stomach, her breathing increasing in momentum as he intensified his caresses, until suddenly she was openly panting. The panting intensified to a hoarse moan as their bodies joined, they ignored the creaking of the old-fashioned bed. She felt his strength boring into her and leaving her. Eventually, their passion spent, they lay motionless, arms entwined on the crumpled bed. Jameson stole a glance at his wristwatch. He had things to do. He moved cautiously so as to avoid waking her again, and dressed quickly. He left the room as stealthily as his numbed senses would allow and returned to his own room. He now had business to attend to. To his surprise the room was empty.

There was no sign of Inspector Fisher and no sign that he'd even been there. One glance at the register downstairs would have shown Fisher which room they were booked into. Peter Jameson could only wait. He sat in the chair, pulled an eiderdown from one bed about his shoulders and dozed.

The telephone screamed in his brain, jolting him into wakefulness. He picked it up. 'I'm not slept out yet,' he was tempted to say, and was glad he didn't.

"What the hell are you doing?" It was Commander Burt's voice.

Jameson glances at his watch, it was past midday.

"Well, I can't do very much yet, I'm waiting for Inspector Fisher to get back here."

"That aircraft has just left to return to the States," barked the Commander, "and the only reason I knew about it was because somebody at Yeadon's got a few brains and remembered that our 'firm' enquired about our American cousins."

"Oh!" was all a startled Jameson could first manage, but he went on. "I am very sorry Commander," Peter Jameson now said deliberately, "but I have been waiting to hear from Fish, and for the 'back-up' which your department told me last night was on its way."

Commander Burt was in no mood for arguments.

"Jameson," he said, "I sent you up to the wilds of Yorkshire because I thought, mistakenly it seems, that you, out of all the people I could call on, were the most resourceful! It seems I was wrong!"

Peter Jameson was silent.

"Are you there?"

"Yes sir," replied Peter Jameson. "Sorry, I was thinking – there's something wrong."

"What do you mean, something? I know there's something wrong," barked the Commander. "I want you tell me what it is."

"Well, I've not heard of or seen Fisher since I saw him leave the train from London at five last evening. And he hasn't come back to the hotel where he knew we were booked in."

"Stay there," was the reply. "I'll find out where the Americans stayed last night, maybe Fisher's there. I'll get back to you."

The line went dead.

Jameson looked at the now silent telephone receiver in his hand, before replacing it. It had been quite a night. He slowly took off all his clothes, dumped them on his unused bed and made his way to the bathroom, pausing only to switch on the radio set. He had almost finished shaving when the lunchtime news bulletin commenced. The announcer began with the economic news which was bad. The pound had lost another 4 cents against the dollar, and now stood at an all time low. The Prime Minister was meeting with the Chancellor of the Exchequer the day after tomorrow. 'Typical,' Jameson said to himself. 'Why leave it for another day? Why couldn't he just go round and see the Chancellor right away? Afterall, No 10 and No 11 Downing Street were next door to one another. What a way to run a country!' He towelled himself savagely, dressed himself and sat back waiting to be contacted. It was after 6 p.m. when there was a knock at his door. The two back-up men had arrived. In the meantime, a search of the hotels in Bradford by the local police had revealed that their quarry had left very early that morning, and so far had vanished without trace.

"Ah, that could explain the disappearance of Inspector Fisher," said Jameson. "If he's following them he won't have had a chance to phone in, that is assuming he's following them."

He began to trace circles on the map with his finger to denote the radius of possible distances travelled.

"They'd just about had time to leave the country at the furthest point, which is Dover."

The shorter of the two back-up men sniffed and said:

"That's if they've left the country. Yeadon immigration said neither Coggin nor HH were aboard the private jet, so they could be lost in any major city. But its your case old buddy, we were just sent to assist in observation and surveillance."

The telephone rang. Yorkshire television wanted to know whether 11 a.m. would be too early for Peter Jameson to interview the Chief Constable, the man whose efforts had succeeded in the apprehension of two IRA leaders. It had made big headlines a month ago.

Due to the events of the past twenty-four hours Peter Jameson had temporarily forgotten he was in Bradford to do a TV interview. He told them he'd call back after he'd contacted the Chief Constable by telephone. No sooner had he replaced the receiver than it rang again. This time it was Maria from the hotel bar. She'd been waiting patiently for him for an hour for the dinner date which they had arranged.

"If you don't get here soon I shall be too drunk to go out," she said, "I've already had four large ones."

"Who's counting" he chuckled, "you'll need all of them and more to get your strength back after last night, not to mention this morning."

"Yes, that was very naughty of you," she said. "I've felt half dead all day."

"Listen," said Jameson, "two friends of mine have just arrived and will be joining us." He could picture her making a face into the phone, but said, "We'll be right down," and replaced the receiver.

The atmosphere was tense throughout the evening but if Maria noticed it she said nothing. The three men expected the interruption of the telephone call from London that never came. Finally, Peter Jameson could stand the tension no longer. They were at the coffee stage when he excused himself, went over to the reception desk and gave the clerk the telephone number which would connect Jameson with the control centre of the undercover section of special branch.

"723-9686," the guarded female voice answered, "which company do you require?"

"Special Features, British Broadcasting Corporation," he replied.

This was his code, the unique code which identified him. Each agent had a different code, which they and only they knew, and even these codes were frequently changed.

There was a short pause as the operator checked the code list beside her. Her finger moved swiftly to the letter 'S'. Yes, there it was, Special Features, BBC, with the name Peter Jameson beside it.

"I'm putting you through to that Department, Mr Jameson," she said.

Jameson made a mental note to have that operator disciplined. He had not given his name and had he been making the call in other circumstances it could have meant the difference between life and death. His life and his death! Operations had heard nothing from Inspector Fisher, but they assured Peter Jameson that the moment anything came in, whatever time of day or night, he would be informed, and with this he had to be content.

His sleep, however, remained undisturbed, and it was nine-thirty next morning before the telephone rang. This was it, he thought. But it was not; it was Commander Burt now sounding seriously worried as there had been no word from Fisher.

"I'm coming back to London, Commander," Jameson said, "as soon as I've done my interview. There are a number of things I've got to discuss with you. I'll leave your two men to handle anything that turns up here and to search this area. Obviously, Coggin hasn't been seen?"

"No, he's not been seen at all," replied the Commander, "but we could pick up Anna Dubric and put the squeeze on her? You know we haven't any real evidence against Coggin. And your evidence wouldn't be very strong. Why Fisher didn't give you the exposed film when he gave you the Minox I fail to understand."

"The only thing I can think is that he changed the film, sir, and slipped the exposed one into his pocket," replied Peter Jameson.

"Right Commander, if you'll pencil me in your diary, I'll be at your office in Regents Park by four-thirty. I'll use the tradesman's entrance."

He put the phone down.

What had happened to Fisher?

He had a few thoughts buzzing around in his head and not one of them was pleasant. It now seemed unlikely that Fisher was free: in one and a half days he ought to have found some way to contact the department. This left two possibilities: that he had been captured or that he had been disposed of permanently. Jameson hoped fervently that it was not the latter. He'd grown to like Fisher, he was a good policeman who'd started on the beat and worked his way up through his aptitude. This aptitude had been recognised and he'd been transferred to the Secret Service. Unlike himself, who'd been brought in by the department to do one specific job, when they needed a 'front' who knew radio. As a radio disc jockey, he fitted the job description. But equally important the same person needed to know his way around the American military bases in Europe. Jameson, too, had once kept himself alive selling family bibles on the American bases. So Special Branch had trained him to do the job. This he had passed so successfully that he'd been kept on after its completion. He had very little say in the matter, he'd signed the Official Secrets Act and Commander Burt had his own methods in terms of persuasion. Some members of Burt's highly professional section resented the presence of Peter Jameson, but not Fisher. He'd been assigned to work with him and had given all the help his experience would allow. Jameson wished now he'd looked at the documents in Coggin's briefcase more thoroughly. But Fisher had photographed them, all he could really remember were some details in connection with four names, Lord Lampton, Lord Gilhauley, Nigel Warrington and Jane Lumley. He forced himself back from his mental wanderings and concentrated on the job at hand. He had an important interview before the all-revealing TV cameras in less than half an hour.

*

The Yorkshire Pullman Express pulled into Kings Cross one minute ahead of the published timetable, but the traffic condition on the Euston and Marylebone Roads leading to Regents Park was even worse than usual and therefore it was almost 5 p.m. before Peter Jameson was ushered into the great man's office. The Commander looked up as Peter Jameson entered. With the worry he was experiencing over the disappearance of Fisher and its implications, he seemed slightly unsure of himself.

"We've got the Dubric woman downstairs," he said. "Been here for about half an hour. She thinks she's here in connection with forged travellers cheques at the club. Here we can listen in."

He pressed a switch underneath his desk and the room was filled with sound.

'But you must have had some idea,' the woman interrogator was saying.

'No, no, no,' cried Anna Dubric, 'nothing.'

They listened for some moments to the standard police probing procedure. The questions were asked, and then re-asked, the answers given were checked and re-checked. Accusations made and denied. It was a deliberate procedure to get an accused into a high state of anxiety so they became vulnerable. Jameson motioned to the Commander to turn down the sound. The Commander switched the speaker off.

"I think she's about ready," he said.

"What would you say if I saw her?" Jameson asked the Commander.

It came as a surprise to him when Commander Burt agreed readily, as he knew the Commander did not approve of his womanising ways, and he was not so naïve as to think the Chief of the Secret Service did not have a fairly accurate picture of their past relationship. But he was clever enough to let his operatives use their own personalities to achieve results, despite his personal views. This was one of the strengths of the man and it inspired confidence.

Jameson went on, "It's time, I think, for a positive approach. All her suspicions will return as soon as I walk into that room. What she might half suspect when she sees me is that I'm after Coggin and then she'll feed me a red herring, but we'll have to risk it."

"Risk it nothing," came back the sharp retort from Burt. "If it goes wrong I'll put her under wraps until this thing is over."

He pressed a buzzer on his intercom to make the arrangements for the two WPCs to be withdrawn from the interview room. Anna Dubric sat elbows on the table, face in cupped hands, dejectedly alone in the bare room starkly lit by the single electric light bulb suspended from the ceiling. The bare, pale green walls seemed to reflect the disconsolate spirits of those who were interrogated within them. A twelve foot square room gives the feeling of such claustrophobia, especially when its only small window is barred and shuttered. Jameson watched her through the specially constructed one-way viewing panel for some moments, trying to decide how involved in this whole business she was. The man who'd been recruiting winos to set off bombs had reported to her, and she certainly knew something of Coggin's activities. None of the blackmail pictures he'd seen had featured her, but then he'd seen but a few. He decided it was time for him to find out. She looked up as the door opened and he entered.

"Hello, Anna," he said, trying to keep his voice as low key as possible, knowing that every word was being recorded. Her face showed an expression of amazement and then changed to bewilderment as, impulsively, she jumped up, knocking the chair over, and started towards him. He stopped her before she could fling her arms around him, and taking hold of her wrists he firmly placed them by her sides.

"Anna," he said soothingly, but firmly, "sit down, we're going to have a little chat. You could be in very serious trouble and I did not come here to bail you."

"But I don't understand," she began, "I thought..."

"I know what you thought," he interrupted her, "that you were involved in cheque frauds. Well, it's not that – or at least if you are, we don't know about it."

"You said we. You mean you're with the police?"

"Not quite, Secret Service, Special Branch." He was playing it by ear and decided to come directly to the point. "I want you to tell me everything you know about Mark Coggin."

She gasped, and he continued.

"And I don't want any lies, or info withheld. We know quite a lot and can check the accuracy of your answers. Be very careful. This next half an hour could play a crucial part in the next ten years of your life. Tell me everything even if you think it is bad news and let me decide how bad. OK?"

His speech must have impressed her because she was silent, first looking at him for inspiration and then when none came she circled the small room before re-seating herself.

"What do I call you now? Captain?" She said nervously, "I've been dreading this for a long time."

"No, not captain, I don't have a rank only a grade. Just call me what you've always called me."

He hoped that she wouldn't call him anything embarrassing, but he need not have feared, Anna was too tactful for that, and besides, she was on his side now!

"I've known Mark Coggin for many years now," she began, "and I know that he ships arms to Ireland."

This was a most promising start.

"How?" he asked.

"Air freight."

"How do you know? And which way?"

"When I came over from Czechoslovakia it was after the failed revolution. We were betrayed by the Americans," an angry note creeping into her voice. "I was a young girl then, just eighteen years old, and my mother paid all her savings to have me smuggled into Poland and then on to a cargo boat for England. The captain was an American, but the man who met us when we docked in London was Mark Coggin."

"Anna, I'd love to hear the story of your life some other time, but how do you know about the arms route?" he asked.

"It's a mixture of guessing and facts. When I arrived I had no money and my English was not as good as it is now. I was taken from the ship by Mark Coggin to an old lady and I stayed at her house in Wandsworth for two years. I heard nothing from my mother but I thought she had paid for all of this. I was wrong."

"Anna, get to the point."

"I was just about to if you stop interrupting," she said haughtily. "The day I left school there was a knock on the door. I opened it. There stood Mark Coggin. He told me a little about his organisation and how he had a two-year investment in me and it was time I earned my living. The rest you can probably guess. I became a high-class call girl."

"And this is what you do now?"

"No, Mark Coggin's business expanded two years ago when he began his arms dealing. His girls now have different jobs. They keep his contacts 'happy'."

"I'm beginning to get–"

She went on as if not hearing him.

"At first I hardly realised what was happening to me. The life wasn't so bad once I got used to it. But I gradually discovered what a cruel man Mark Coggin was and that guns and things were coming here. By this time he had so much on me that I just had to go on, and then there was my mother. He told me he could have her arrested by the party in Prague and tortured, thrown into jail and even made to disappear."

"What's your function now?" asked Jameson.

He knew Commander Burt would be listening to every revelation with baited breath, the girl was really telling a story.

"I steer the girls towards the contacts Mark Coggin gives me, and then give him the information they give me. My function now is that of a blackmail madam. When I said Coggin was cruel he's even more than that, he's evil. You should see some of that blackmail stuff. Sometimes these people have done just little things wrong but he makes them do things which make it worse and worse for them while he gains."

She was working her voice into a hateful tone now.

"Because Mark Coggin is on such good terms with 'the party' in Prague he could get my mother out; he's been promising it for... oh, I don't know how long, but it never happens. But he has made me do things I would never have done by threatening what he could have done to my mother."

"The route," Peter Jameson prompted her gently.

"Oh yes. From Prague you go as the freight driver's mate, it's not unusual in my country for women to do this work. The freight truck is unloaded in Italy and flown to Beauvais where it is re-labelled and flown to Lydd."

"Lydd, here in Kent?"

"Yes."

"You told me a few minutes ago your information on this route was a mixture of facts and guesswork. Explain to me what you meant."

She replied, "I keep in contact with all the girls. That's part of my job. Coggin has no direct contact with them. They see him around the clubs, but they think he's just another fool with too much money. But a few months ago he brought a girl over from Czechoslovakia, I talked to her about how she came here and she told me this story. The freight company uses old World War II Dakotas, and a special passenger seat was installed in the tail of the plane. She told me the freight was stacked all around her. She said that between Italy and France the trip took hours and hours so out of curiosity she looked at the labels on the packages – they were labelled medical instruments, and were addressed to a firm in Belfast, she couldn't remember the name, Sharing something."

"Go on," he prompted her.

"As they were landing in Beauvais the aircraft hit a cross wind and lurched sideways and the wing almost hit the runway. She said she was terrified, but the aircraft bounced sideways and it seemed one tyre blew out. The freight shifted and one long box split. Through the crack in the box protruded the barrel of a rifle. She couldn't believe her eyes but pushed it back into the box and said nothing. After the wheel was replaced they took off again for England. In England she got off the plane and was taken by the pilot or navigator, she didn't know who, through a hangar to the car park. There were no officials, nothing. From there they just got in a car and drove to London.

"That's some story, Anna," he said quietly, when she'd finished. "Now look, I'm going to have to leave you here for a while but I'm going to have a pot of tea sent in for you and a WPC will take a statement, but don't worry, I'll come back. OK?"

"I'd sooner you sent me a large Scotch," she replied, some of her old spirit returning. "But I'll put in writing what I've told you."

He tapped on the tiny window of the door to be let out and gave swift instructions outside to one of the two uniformed WPCs guarding the door.

The door to Commander Burt's oak-panelled office closed silently behind him and Peter Jameson made his way across the thick pile carpet to the vacant visitor's chair as indicated to him by the chief's gesture. The Commander was listening to the recorded interview and at the same time signing letters and memos which he took from a mountain of files stacked at one end of his desk.

"From a purely professional point of view," he said when the recording had finished, "your interrogation technique was about as mistake-ridden as any that I've eavesdropped upon in a long time. You were too friendly, asked no trick questions, no names, dates, places, times..."

"You'll get more from the trained cop taking her statement now," interrupted Jameson. "My job was to get her going!" He scowled. "And I've not finished with her yet. Anyway, I believe her. Her story matches with what we know."

The Commander raised his hand, halting the continuing protests mounting on Jameson's lips.

"I'm only telling you what you should have done, going by the book. But one advantage you have over the trained policeman is that you're not a trained policeman and you do things from instinct rather than because you've had techniques rammed into you over the years. No, I think Anna Dubric would have wriggled, squirmed and lied and we'd probably never have got the full truth from her if you hadn't been to bed with her and if we'd followed the book. But in your amateurish way you'll get her to cough the lot! Which is what I thought would happen."

Jameson couldn't resist saying, "You could say, sir, that some intimate knowledge of the lady had advantages!"

Burt let the crack pass without comment.

"I think we can do a deal with Miss Dubric," he said. "What she has done, although highly illegal, was very much because Coggin blackmailed her into it. Nasty piece of work this Coggin. Now a good barrister might get her off with three years, or if she was unlucky she'd get a five to eight year stretch and then be deported."

"Then she would be well in it if we deported her back home!" Exclaimed Jameson. "Communists don't take kindly to their young citizens blowing the country unauthorised."

The Commander continued: "I think I could promise that she wouldn't be prosecuted in return for her complete cooperation. Think she'll go along with that?" And he added meticulously, "After all, you're the one with the intimate knowledge of the lady!"

Jameson smiled briefly, appreciating the by-play.

"She'd be a fool if she doesn't."

"Very well," said Commander Burt getting to his feet. "Let's go and see her."

*

Jameson opened the door for him.

Anna Dubric welcomed the pot of tea which arrived shortly after Peter Jameson's departure, and she was grateful for the fact that the WPC who came with it to take her statement was experienced but kind. She noticed her hands were trembling as she poured herself a cup of tea. She was scared. She had not meant to be as frank with Peter Jameson as she had been, but he had been so disarming and with his direct approach she had not had time to think, and had blurted out what had been pent up inside her for years. Now she could be in serious trouble, she thought. They might even send her back to Czechoslovakia. She had known that Mark Coggin had been committing acts of treason and she'd helped him, however unwillingly. She shivered at the thought of being sent back.

Anna trembled at the thought of even one interrogation by the Communist Secret Police. She drew on her cigarette and, as she answered the WPC's questions mechanically, she thought ironically how the Western World did not know the real Czech people. There is a Peoples Party but the only people who have any say in an Iron Curtain country are the members of the Communist Party. Even those who want to become members of the party cannot just join it. A prospective member is selected and investigated by the presidium and if they agree that the candidate has potential then he or she is invited to join. However, once a member you become a privileged person. You get on in your job and as you gain status within the party you acquire property, wealth and you live well. You can even make unopposed visits to the West, but you are never free and are under constant investigation. That is the true meaning of a police state. When you die everything you have acquired reverts back to the State. It is impossible to make bequests, your bank account is emptied and even gifts such as jewellery given to you by your family are re-possessed. Anna hoped fervently she would not be sent back to the country she had left behind all those years ago. Similar thoughts continued long after she'd signed her statement and the WPC had left.

Her broodings were interrupted as the key turned in the lock of the interview room, and the door opened. In strode Commander Burt closely followed by Peter Jameson.

"Good afternoon, Miss Dubric," he said in a level, formal voice which gave no hint of what he had in mind. "And I see you've been given some tea. I'll bet that was young Jameson's idea. Thoughtful fellow, Jameson."

Anna had yet to speak and as the three sat at the table the Commander introduced himself.

"Jameson has informed you of the gravity of your situation?"

The girl nodded. Peter Jameson could not help feeling sorry for her, she looked terrified. He glanced sideways at Commander Burt, the expression on whose face remained impassive. He kept quiet, knowing better than to interrupt Commander Burt's carefully planned approach.

"What is going to happen to me?" Anna asked.

It was then that Commander Burt dropped his bombshell.

"I hope," he said, "that in about one hour's time you will walk out of this building a free woman. But that depends on you."

If he had said she'd been selected as America's first lady he could not have achieved a more dramatic effect. She opened her astonished mouth to speak but it just hung open with words refusing to come out.

Peter Jameson decided it was time for him to intervene.

"Look Anna," he said, "we, that is Commander Burt and myself, want Coggin and we want you to help us get him. What the Commander is saying is that you work with us and we won't press charges against you."

"I'm dreaming," she said.

Jameson went on: "This deal we are offering you is no bed of roses. Make no mistake, it'll be dangerous. We'll get Coggin with or without you but you can make it much easier for us."

Anna spoke slowly, directing her words at both of them.

"Gentlemen," she said in the foreign formal way of speaking English, "you do not comprehend how much pleasure I shall take in working for you. Ever since I was in England, nearly ten years ago, this Mark Coggin has been pushing me around. I tried to tell you, Peter, that he was an evil man. Yes," she gave a hard smile, "it will be a pleasure. A great pleasure."

"Well then," said the Commander, "shall we adjourn to my office?"

The trio's footsteps clattered hollowly along the parquet-floor corridor which led to Commander Burt's office. For security reasons his office was kept locked when empty and therefore it was not unusual that Thompson, Commander Burt's secretary, was seated upon the chair outside, provided for that purpose. Upon her lap was a red folder, the colour classification showed that its contents required immediate action.

"This came in five minutes ago, sir," she said.

"Well then, what is it?" said the Commander brusquely as he busied himself unlocking and opening the door.

"I think you should see it for yourself, sir," said Thompson. "It's about Inspector Fisher. It's not good news I'm afraid."

Expressionlessly he took the folder from her and read the foolscap telex the file contained. Following upon which he examined the wired picture , the quality was poor as a result of Yorkshire's old-fashioned wire-processing system, but it was unmistakably Fisher. He shook his head as he faced them across his large desk around which they'd gathered.

"I'm afraid it's the worst news I can give you. I have to tell you Fisher's dead."

The words struck like a blow behind Peter Jameson's heart.

Although he had felt something must have happened to Fisher he had been fervently hoping for better news than this by the hour.

"How did it happen?" he said to Burt, trying to sound unemotional.

Already in his own mind he had formulated a picture. Fisher had been after two people, Coggin and the mysterious HH. Therefore, it stood to reason one of them, possibly both of them had discovered and disposed of Fisher. Silently the Commander handed the telex to Jameson, the facts revealed themselves coldly before his eyes. A violent blow to the side of the head had brought about the death, and the police mortician's examination had shown that the bleak hillside in the Dales near Knaresborough, where a shepherd's dog had found the body, was not the place of death. The established time of death was between 10 p.m. and twelve midnight of the day Fisher and Jameson had arrived in Bradford.

Commander Burt spoke: "OK. We are now after a police killer, but we are also involved in something much bigger. I had a feeling when these London bombings first started to become a little more sophisticated than was hitherto the case, that there was a whiff of outside influence around. Having a suspicious mind I suspected communist influence. I now believe it goes even further than that."

"You mean the communists have joined forces with somebody like the IRA?" Said Jameson.

"Or worse," replied Burt. "Commercial people. Recall what I said to you at Lords, Jameson? About commercial interests stretching beyond the sale of arms in Ireland and increasingly now the mainland."

"Bloody hell! It's deadly, sir, even the thought of it."

As Peter Jameson continued to listen to the Commander's theorising, he wondered just how much Anna Dubric should be told of the whole affair. With Fisher now dead and the film missing she knew a lot that they did not and she could be the key to the unlocking of a major part of Coggin's organisation. The appearance of the late Inspector must have thrown Coggin into one hell of a panic for him to be killed and then Coggin's disappearance must mean that Fisher had been caught after he'd found something out. The question was, what? Jameson had a feeling Coggin would head for Prague, but would he take the Lydd, Beauvais, Prague route to get there? Jameson felt he would need to short-circuit that route and get Coggin before he got to Prague.

Anna spoke. "Commander, I told you downstairs I'd help you in every way possible to catch Mark Coggin."

Now she was no longer scared, her voice carried the low-pitched ring of confidence and mystique that non-continentals find so attractive in continental women, and the way she strung her words into sentences would always reveal that she was not British.

"Now it seems he has killed one of your policemen?"

"We don't know it for sure. But it seems fairly certain that if he didn't he knows something about it," said Commander Burt. "From the information you have given us we've now established a definite link between the communists and Coggin's arms dealing and others. This places them in the position of supporting the IRA and other illegal organisations and of creating an activity of their own which they claim to be the responsibility of one group or another."

Jameson spoke: "There's a lot you must be able to tell us Anna, but first let us tell you our story from the beginning and then you fill us in on any gaps."

He told her in some detail and when he had finished she outlined what had been her role. It seemed Coggin had been adroit in the manipulation of Anna. She did not know about his involvement in bombings but knew he supplied arms to terrorists.

She had unknowingly acted as a message centre for Coggin's activity. She controlled the girls for Coggin and therefore learned of the blackmail secrets but thought he used them to gain business advantages.

"How about Coggin's companies? Bensons?" asked Jameson. "Do you have the run of the place?" He looked at the Commander. "Because we could use somebody in there!"

The Commander nodded as Anna replied:

"Yes, I go there twice a week."

"I think to have things appear natural, Anna, you should go there as before. It will be normal for you to try to be in contact with Coggin," said Jameson. "And you must try to keep your behaviour as normal as you can. I know you've never tried to find out much about the organisation's activities before, but now it's very important that you keep your eyes and ears open and get us a lead on where we can find Coggin. I'll keep in touch with you at the Fanlight Club and your place."

Anna looked excited. "I'm glad for this chance you have given me Commander."

"It'll be dangerous," replied Commander Burt, "so if you find out anything don't take any chances, get in touch with Jameson immediately and let us handle it."

And with a wicked twinkle in his eye he concluded, "You stick to what you're good at!"

*

Anna tried to compose herself as she entered Berkeley Square House, in Berkeley Square. She was afraid that her face and voice would give her away when she asked the young office girl, "Where's Mark?" but it didn't. The reply came back quite naturally:

"He's left on a buying trip abroad."

"What, without even telling me?"

"Afraid so," an American voice said from the open doorway.

She spun around to face the owner of the voice.

"I'm taking over here for a while ma'am, and I guess you must be Anna."

"That's right", she replied, her voice trailing away.

"Guess you didn't know the organisation's extensive Stateside activities, huh?"

Something in Anna's brain made a warning sound. The arrival of the American, together with a colleague as it subsequently turned out, was altogether too pat. It was phoney. Coggin disappears with the immensely wealthy but mysterious HH and less than a week later Americans appear at Coggin's HQ blandly implying that Coggin was just part of a very much larger outfit and that they are running the show from now on. This one seemed totally aware of Anna's role in the business. He looked like a well-fed toad, wearing a dark business suit, double-breasted, covering up his three stone weight problem, and black expensive pointed shoes affected so frequently by Italian Americans. It therefore came as a surprise when he drawled:

"The name's Joe O'Hara. Anna, you wanna tell me what those girls of yours have bin doin'?"

Anna's brain raced like a freshly wound stopwatch. Here was her chance for some swift results. The American Joe O'Hara was not Coggin and because of this she could fool him into believing that she was trustworthy.

She smiled at him impudently, "You know, Joe," she said, "I think I'm going to like working with you."

Chapter 7

Undercover Activities

Anna Dubric had no illusions about the dangerous game she was playing with these two Americans, and her subterfuge could only be very short term. As soon as one of them made contact with Coggin and mention was made of her she would almost certainly be exposed. In all probability they would discover that she was working against them and retribution would then be swift. Strangely enough she didn't care and she was thriving on the excitement. For years she had drifted along with little purpose in her life and now for the first time she felt she was doing something important and worthwhile.

The dreaded (for Anna) but vital (for Jameson) phone call came halfway through the afternoon. It was from Brown's Hotel, Vienna. By sheer chance it was she who answered it and not the dilatory office girl whom Anna planned to fire forthwith. The operator informed Anna Dubric that it was Mark Coggin.

He was startled to hear her voice.

"Is that Anna?" he said, in surprise.

"Yes."

"Where's Sally? What are you doing at the office today?"

She decided to attempt to bluff it out with him.

"Sally's sick and I came to see you, of course, only to be told that you'd gone off on business for a couple of months or so."

There was a pause at the other end of the phone and then Coggin said cautiously: "Is everything alright there?"

"Yes, of course, Mark" replied Anna. "Why shouldn't it be?"

If Mark Coggin was fishing he wasn't going to get anything out of her, but she'd do some cautious fishing of her own.

"Where are you, Mark? It's not like you to just take off!"

"Oh, something came up while I was up north. Listen, there should be two Americans arriving any time."

"Yes, they're already here, O'Hara and Sweeney. That's one reason I'm still here, they wanted someone mature around. I expect you want to speak to them."

"Oh, er... OK. Yes, put me on to them."

With some fear in her heart Anna pressed the button which would link Coggin with the men in the adjoining office. Every instinct told her to get up and run. It could only be a question of time now, she thought, before the door to that adjoining office would open and one, probably both of the Americans, would enter and put paid to her brief spying career.

"Pull yourself together, Anna," Dubric told herself angrily. "What would a proper spy do?" She asked herself. But was she a proper spy? A spy would listen in, but not get caught at it! She smiled to herself... No *she* would not be caught listening in, but the listening would be done. She would enlist the services of the useful friend Jameson had provided her with. Her immediate panic at least temporarily halted, Anna Dubric pressed a tiny red record button concealed under her desk. This was connected to the sealed, remote, miniature tape machine, surreptitiously hidden away in the locked bottom drawer of the reception desk! At a casual glance the machine had the appearance of a Winston Churchill statue in the form of a paper weight, but it would silently be "Big Brothering' all conversations made on Mark Coggin's private telephone line, for a period in excess of two hours. Jameson had had made up a whole family of such famous statesmen as eavesdropping devices, unmodified, their purpose was straightforward unseen audio surveillance, triggered in normal operation by digital activation. 'Q' department were tickled pink by Jameson's suggestion that the nostrils of General de Gaulle's famous 'honker' be used to house tiny 'micro' units which were the sensitive pick-ups for the surveillance, so much so that this theme was adopted as a feature in all the department's similar eavesdropping devices.

The minutes ticked by and Anna sat with her eyes riveted to the light glowing on the telephone extension which denoted that the telephone conversation was in progress. Her suspense lasted for fifteen minutes and then quite suddenly the light on the telephone was extinguished. She waited, her nerves tense, and she continued to wait. In the end her nerves could stand the strain not one moment longer. She knocked on the adjoining door and went in. O'Hara had his feet on Mark Coggin's desk and Sweeney was straddling the turned-round visitors chair. Their faces registered no special emotion and she said lamely:

"I'm going home now fellows. Shall I see you at the club later?"

"Oh, sure!" said Sweeney with a crooked grin. "We shall want to look over the property."

She forced herself to smile back rather as men do when embarking on a dirty joke and threw her right hand up in a mock salute, "Yes, sir," she said, "property for inspection, sir. Black girls or white girls?" Then she joined in the ribald laughter and left the room.

*

Peter Jameson answered the door to his Knightsbridge flat. It was, as he expected, the delivery man from the Piccadilly store, Fortnum and Mason. The delivery man held a box containing the six bottles of champagne Jameson had ordered a mere hour ago.

Mechanically Jameson signed the delivery sheet and flicked a fifty pence piece to the delivery man, to this he added a crisp fiver. Then he carried the valuable cargo into his kitchen and methodically stowed it in the 'fast cool' section of his large refrigerator. Anna would be here within the hour and she'd earned a small celebration. Events were moving more speedily than he could have dared hope. Anna's guarded telephone call to him during her lunch break had sent his spirits soaring. O'Hara had taken Anna's bait and without knowing it, had filled in for her the many blank spaces in her knowledge of Mark Coggin's activities. But best of all Jameson knew of Mark Coggin's whereabouts and that gentleman was already under discreet but watertight surveillance. Anna was even aware of the location of a storage depot in the tiny seaside village near Hythe in Kent. Along this part of the coast were situated a number of medical equipment manufacturers. Coggin's illegal shipments mingled innocently with the regular freight which was collected by the German freight vessel twice monthly for delivery to the Republic of Ireland.

*

When Anna Dubric had gone, the two Irish Americans looked at one another smiling speculatively.

"Well now," Sweeney said. "I think raisin' hell in the IRA through this office is gonna have better prospects than in the Windy City, and good extra curricular possibilities, Joe! Whadda you reckon? It's pretty shrewd eh? HH havin' an Irish *woman* runnin' the bombings from Dublin, with a diplomatic call-girl cover operation? So's when Mrs McGuinness comes over here to London to put it about a bit, like Coggin jus' told us she does, people think the bitch is just another high class Irish whore! I guess you'd call that shrewd market research," he chuckled. "HH sure is a clever bastard having his own insider woman right in the heart of the IRA and her husband secretly working for their political wing. But you know something else, O'Hara? We're probably the only American tourists in London who don't have to worry about running into a terrorist bomb! Even Capone couldn't say that huh? Then we got Anna," Sweeney went on. "Big bouncy Anna, she's sure got all her equipment in the right places ain't she? And boy does she show out... Jesus! She's got boobs bigger than bowling balls. Did ya' notice?"

"I noticed," said O'Hara nodding and smiling. "Coggin told us we could trust her 'cos he's got some kind of hold on her. It's a good thing she fired that other dumb broad," he said meaningfully. "She's got far bigger qualifications. What hold d'ya reckon Coggin's got on her?"

"Blackmail of course, Joe? Doesn't that form the basis of all big business! Now I'm a bum and tit man," Sweeney said as if staking a claim, "so she'll do for me!"

A boys-in-the-boardroom smile was exchanged, Sweeney concluding, "We, too, need an insider in the Fanlight Club, Joe."

"You're a bum alright, Bob," chuckled the fat one, "but if HH wants us to tell this Mrs McGuinness, the Irish/London operation goes through this office from now on," he shrugged his shoulders. "What's the best way of doin' things?" He thought for a moment before he continued, then as if thinking out loud said, "We get her to come over here for some serious bomb placement co-ordination... right! 'Cos that's what these Irish are lackin' in, co-ordination... then," O'Hara said making a descriptive hand gesture, "we make up a foursome, and that way get closer to HH's 'insider' as well, right?"

"With what she knows," Sweeney said thoughtfully, "and Coggin out of the way, we could start our own blackmail division!"

The two Americans were in thought but briefly before O'Hara said enthusiastically, "Now you're cookin' on gas, Bob!"

He said jokingly patronising, "You wanna' call her, Mr Sweeney, or shall I?" This is gonna' be an important phone call, so business before pleasure mind!"

"No, best you do it, Joe. I reckon you will kinda' like the idea of telling her about the promotional ideas we got. And right under her old man's English nose. You know he's too busy playing politics, and having his nooky with Labour Party chicks, to bother about a small matter like his wife gettin' knocked up!" Sweeney ended with his throaty chuckle.

"She's married to an Englishman?" O'Hara questioned. "McGuiness sounds pretty Irish to me."

"Not just an Englishman," Sweeney said, "but an English Lord, an English turncoat who is a very secret political weapon for the IRA... Now can you see the Irish/American Money Line, Joe? And how do I know all this?" Sweeney now smiled smugly. "That information came straight form a fund-raising, American Senator's mouth no less, and one who's pretty close to HH. One of the HH bodyguards, a footballer I know from way back, told me. This Senator was at Yale with HH, and", he said meaningfully, "they're pretty close that lot from Yale. You know, fraternity pacts, amateur dramatics, gang bangs, and all that stuff. Yeah, HH the character actor. Does that surprise you when you think about some of the Howard Hughes dramatics he's had us pull? So we'll pull one now. Don't piss around when you call Dublin, Joe, blow her lots of shit! Tell her how close we are to HH! We've got a battle to plan, Chicago-style," Sweeney said spiritedly. "I'll sit in reception and listen in to your line of chat. We'll call it Irish blarney, mid-west Chicago-style, Anna's gone and it'll make sure nobody else listens in, me sittin' there! Bomb placement, they ain't seen nuttin' here yet! HH sure knew what he was doin' when he appointed two Chicago men to run a bombing operation. We got the experience!"

*

Anna Dubric left Berkeley Square House anxiously seeking a taxi. It was not until she became level with Jack Barclay's, the Rolls Royce main dealer, that one arrived with its 'for hire' sign lighted up. She got in, giving Peter Jameson's Knightsbridge address. She was looking forward to visiting him at his place.

It had been quite a day and she thought she'd coped very well with things and was hoping for some well-earned praise from him. The taxi negotiated the crowded Park Lane rush hour traffic by illegal use of the bus lane and she was soon outside his flat. The low-pitched buzzer gave three short bursts. That would be Anna, thought Jameson and before opening the front door he went into his kitchen and to the ice bucket where there resided half a bottle of champagne. He poured a glass, thinking to himself, I'll show her a bit of style, and he went to open the door and greet her with it in his hand. She looked equally well-dressed in office attire, her rust-coloured trouser suit and the fitted waistcoat showed her figure off to perfection. He held the glass of champagne towards her, and as she accepted it, said:

"And how's my favourite hooker?"

"Oh shut up you, you rat," she answered. "I've retired to work for the British Government for the night." She thrust her shoulders back in mock dramatic pose as she stood beside him. "There you see the biggest pair of brains in the service."

Peter Jameson smiled at her, "I knew those brains showed great promise. Come on in," he said. "I won't argue. But work before play. Tell me all your news."

Chapter 8

No Smoking

Commander Burt sat at his desk mechanically reading and initialling the memos Miss Thompson had efficiently typed. He had not slept at all well the previous night and although his wife knew him well enough, after all these years, not to interfere, she had risked a gentle, "You mustn't take it too hard, dear."

"Take it hard," he snapped. "Of course I take it hard. Do you think I like losing good men? How do you think his wife feels. Just wait until I get my hands on whoever did it."

All the information that Anna Dubric had given them on blackmail victims was now being unobtrusively but carefully investigated. His top secret telephone calls to both the Foreign and Home Secretaries had left them very worried men. It concerned the Home Office more than the Foreign Office, but Burt was an astute civil servant. By involving both offices he eliminated the risk of any cover up. He had had the feeling all along that the Russians were behind those notorious bombings and he'd not been wrong entirely. What did puzzle him was that Coggin's organisation seemed to be totally unconnected with other known Russian operatives in this country.

His scrambled telephone receiver buzzed. He picked it up and punched the scrambling code. There was a fractional pause as the mechanism accepted the code. It was Peter Jameson calling. He listened attentively as Jameson related the incidents of the day, and then said:

"So Coggin's in Vienna? The move to place Dubric objectively has paid off as you thought."

"My guess is that he'll slip across the border to Czechoslovakia," replied Jameson "Is there a station that could..."

"No, I know what you're going to say. It's too risky with the people we've got at our embassy in Vienna. You'll have to go immediately, it's about time you went abroad," he continued. "Your German will be getting a bit rusty. You'd better leave tomorrow. I'll get production to make arrangements."

His finger stabbed the buzzer to summon Miss Thompson.

"You come in here early and everything will have been arranged including your visas for the Iron Curtain countries."

Commander Burt had no sooner replaced the scrambled telephone when it buzzed once more. This time it was the Defence Secretary, he sounded anxious.

"I've just had a meeting with the Home Sec," he began, "about Lord G."

"If you're going to ask me what checks out, George," replied Commander Burt, "officially, nothing yet. But privately I would say it will all fit. And I don't think it'll just be an indecent exposure. I've an idea he's tied into this whole affair much more deeply than just a lavatory indiscretion."

"You mean," asked the Defence Secretary, "that he's a mole working for the Russians?"

"Or worse," Burt said. "George, I've thought a lot about it and since his prep school background doesn't look good I should say that someone discovered that he was a bit bent, put the pressure on him and found that he was not an unwilling subject."

"But Commander Burt, what you are saying is terrible. It amounts to treason in the House of Lords!"

"And I think there's more to come, George, but I've got every available person with top security clearance checking out our information. You know I can only use Special Branch Police detectives to assist my MI5 and 6 agents. Naturally I've taken the appropriate security measures and I'm sending a man abroad tomorrow to bring back one of the men behind this whole business, Mark Coggin, he's a broadcaster."

"A broadcaster?" asked the Minister.

"Yes, it's a good cover for him, isn't it? And, strangely enough, he's very good at the job. We first found him when he was a pirate disc jockey. He did a good job for us, and formed personal links with our Common Market and American friends. After it was over I decided to keep him in the department. I use him when there's a job outside the ordinary. This is one of them. He's good at it. Can't say his name. Hush hush, Douglas."

After he'd finished speaking with the Minister of Defence, Commander Burt wondered just what Jameson had done on this assignment to justify such confidence. He'd sent him to Yorkshire with Fisher and they'd lost Fisher. He'd slept with Dubric and they'd traced Coggin. Oh well, he mused, he was being thrown in at the deep-end again tomorrow.

The Commander lit his pipe and consulted his pocket watch. Seven o'clock, just time to catch the 7.19 from Paddington to his home in Bray. He walked over to the coat stand, picked up his umbrella and, placing his bowler hat upon his head, left his office.

He said hardly a word to Wilkes, the long-suffering chauffeur waiting to take him to the railway station. He was lost in his own thoughts. Who did he really pin his hopes on...? His thoughts were interrupted as they drew up to the kerb at Paddington main line station where he said goodnight to Wilkes. He returned to his thoughts as he headed for the familiar platform three.

Jameson the womaniser. He had proven himself in the past, but what about now? He settled himself into the comfortable railway compartment and looked around him. The men, they were all men, all looked about the same, like penguins. The same suits, shoes, shirts, hats, and the briefcases seemed to denote seniority. The more battered the briefcase, the more senior they were. The usual routine for him: his wife would be waiting for him at the station; the Special Branch man would be feeling bored, but would dutifully follow him home in the carefully disguised Q car. Commander Burt enveloped himself in a cloud of pipe-tobacco smoke. It was the one occasion on which he enjoyed breaking the law. The 'No Smoking' compartment held no terrors for the man travelling on this train. Let any stranger dare say a word!

Solemnly, Commander Burt placed his rolled umbrella with his bowler hat perched on it, on a luggage shelf at such an acute angle as to cover the prohibitive sign.

Chapter 9

An Acquaintance Renewed

Opening his eyes the next morning, Peter Jameson wondered what had hit him! After speaking with his Chief, Anna and he had talked, and drunk a lot of champagne, so much in fact that it had begun to appear that the best bottles were the empty ones! Anna had not wanted to go to her job at the Fanlight Club but as they'd both realised, to have failed to have done so would have appeared instantly suspicious. Fortunately her profession had made her adept at sobering up. After she'd gone he thought, 'You settle down too, fool. If you don't you're going to get yourself killed!' He checked his watch swiftly, knowing that he had more than an hour and a half before he should be at Heathrow, and went into his bathroom. 'Yes,' he said, giving himself a critical look of appraisal in the mirror, 'two Alka Seltzers, I prescribe.'

His head cleared instantly as he began to think what would be happening to him when he arrived in Vienna. Fortunately he knew the city and he had also struck up a friendship with a minor official at the British Embassy the previous year. It was now well into winter and, whilst in England the weather was still quite warm, in Austria more than 1,000 kms from London, he knew it would be freezing. Why was he worrying about what to pack.

He told himself, "I'll buy what I want there. So what, I'm on expenses!"

Cheerfully he got into his BMW parked outside his flat and took the parking ticket which was stuck menacingly on his windscreen and tore it into shreds. Those problems were for Commander Burt's department. He was going abroad to do battle with more important issues than a parking offence. He gently caressed his foot across the accelerator of the BMW and it fired first time as he turned the key in the ignition. Very quickly he was in the flow of the traffic seeking its way in the general direction of Central London.

Mechanically he tried to turn his mind off. He would collect documents and then get on to an ordinary flight to Zurich and after that destiny would take over. He slipped the gear lever into second, put his foot defiantly on the accelerator pedal and at a speed of more than 50mph overtook the stream of traffic struggling lazily into London from the west. He arrived at the offices of Special Branch well ahead of schedules so spent that spare time inspecting Lord Snowdon's aviary at London Zoo. Ghastly, he concluded!

*

Heathrow Airport in the early afternoon was at its busiest. As the black taxi, a special one belonging to the department, dropped Peter Jameson at Queen's Building Terminal 2, the driver winked at him and said, "Don't bother about a tip, sir." And then Jameson was gone, disappearing amongst the throng of travellers who were intent only on their personal problems and jetting themselves and their belongings to their chosen destinations. Jameson noticed the Special Branch man at the exit gate, as he headed for the Swissair flight to Zurich, but to his credit the man gave no show of recognition. He had no way of knowing what Jameson's status was at the present time. The fact that the last time they'd met, Jameson had been returning to England at the end of his assignment and getting red carpet treatment made no difference to this current encounter.

Jameson's route had been decided as air to Zurich, and from there onwards by road to Vienna. Through a 'shell' company of the British Government, a car had been rented for his use from Zurich. He moved casually through the Duty Free section, biding his time before Flight SR 439 would be called. He felt tense but ready for any action necessary. He was ready to take command and make any decision that was required of him. He knew things would not be easy because things never were. He looked about him. Whenever he was at a major airport he was always surprised to see how many people were travelling and this was particularly apparent at London's major airport.

At this moment his flight was called and he proceeded past the smiling ground hostess to the bus that was to take him to the area of the waiting Jet Liner. He wondered idly too, as he listened to the radio control passing its staccato messages to the buses, coaching the passengers to their respective aircraft, why each airline tried to outdo the others in hats for its air hostesses. Did they not realise that their female staff looked neater and certainly more attractive without hats wedged on their heads, as they had to be to counter jet stream! How about one designed in a wind tunnel!

The jet screamed to its crescendo and Jameson went through every passenger's mental nightmare as the plane pounded along the runway during takeoff. And then quite suddenly the engine note dropped and they were climbing quite steeply into the clouds, the undercarriage retracting with a clunk and reducing drag. He released his seat belt when the lighted sign announced permission to do so, and then in common with every smoker in that section of the crowded aircraft he reached for his cigarettes and was soon puffing with relief at his Senior Service, the cigarette of his choice.

The one hour and thirty minute flight passed quickly and the landing lights at Zurich Airport therefore appeared much sooner than Peter Jameson had expected. He had profited from reading the 'In Flight' magazine and had already picked out a smart leather coat from its pages. Although Commander Burt might have a fit when he had to pass the expenditure (in excess of fifteen hundred Swiss Francs), by then it would be too late. He grinned to himself. *Fait accompli*! He prepared himself for the landing which came with the faintest of bumps and then there was the scream of the jets as they reversed to take the weighty aircraft to a manageable pace at which to taxi to within disembarkation distance of the terminal at what was almost certainly one of the world's most important financial capitals.

The customs official eyed Jameson's briefcase containing the Q kit with interest. It looked an expensive, businessman's briefcase, and trained as they were to detect the unusual, in a country so used to attempted currency smuggling and would-be securities frauds, the official opened his mouth to enquire further. As he did so a young man detached himself from the plain clothes officials and softly murmured a few words in the older man's ear. The result was a beaming smile from the hitherto suspicious official and the words "Merci, Monsieur," the scrawled chalk marks were written on to his bags and Jameson was on his way through to the exit without further ado.

"I always enjoy these 'cloak and dagger' jobs," said Harold Rawlingson when they were alone drinking a coffee, "because they never give me any information. I just get a signal, telling me that someone's arriving, and what I have to arrange. No bodies to dispose of this time?"

"No. It's an easy one for you this time," Jameson said. "I'm just passing through to Austria. What car did you get?"

"Nothing too special. It's an Audi on Munich number plates! And," he grinned, "a blower on its engine."

"Ah, that's excellent," said Jameson, "in an emergency that would check out because I lived in Munich for some years and it would seem feasible." He held out his hand, "My friend, I thank you," he said with a smile, and then he left to start the difficult journey across Switzerland, to the enchanting capital city of Austria, Vienna. Leaving Zurich he followed the signs carefully round the lake before settling on the fast autobahn route which would take him to Vienna. Eventually he would leave the modern roads of this clean country. He marvelled at Swiss ingenuity. They could drive twelve mile tunnels through deep mountains, and they could also produce dining areas in hotels capable of competing in modern style and service with the best American standards. They were a very straight and formal race but they would respect a person's banking secrets, provided he was substantial. However, Jameson was on his way to a country with equal beauty. Austria, land of old-fashioned waltzes and the Blue Danube, of Harry Lime and the Zyther, romanticism and intrigue. But mostly, as far as he was concerned, he was going because Mark Coggin was there, and he was after Mark Coggin. He would get him, of that he was sure. Coggin, he believed, had been responsible for the death of his colleague Fisher, and Jameson felt maybe if he had played it slightly differently in Yorkshire, Fisher might still be alive. But maybe he would be dead. However, it was of no use him having regrets now. That was how it had happened and now he was on his own.

He had been so preoccupied by his thoughts that he had not noticed that the speedometer of the car had crept up to 180 kph. He eased his foot from the accelerator. No point in getting a ticket! He forced himself to think about the business in hand. He definitely had problems ahead of him. He would find Coggin if he was still in Vienna. His instructions were to bring him back discreetly. But he needed to extract from Coggin what he knew about the Soviet involvement in the British bomb atrocities. The question for Jameson was how best to do this, and then for Commander Burt how the results could best be shown to the rest of the free world. What the Soviets were now doing was breaking new territory in assisted terrorism.

He crossed the border at Feldkirch. Time for a drink and something to eat. He'd forgotten how hungry he was. He would stop at the next friendly looking *Gasthaus*, he decided. He looked into his driving mirror and observed the lights of the police car behind him become brighter and brighter, until they overtook him. Giving him ample opportunity to stop, the illuminated sign (Poletzei Stop) eased him over on to the hard shoulder of the autobahn. Two formidable white-belted policemen approached his driver's window.

They approached the driver's window with typical continental police caution. Walking with the weight carefully on the balls of their feet ready for instant action, and ten paces could be measured in between them.

The policeman who reached Peter Jameson's window first spoke his carefully rehearsed opening phrase in English:

"Please, Mr Jameson, may I see your car paper, insurance, driving licence, please." He seemed relieved when Jameson replied in German, and he reverted to his native tongue. "And please, your passport."

Examining all four documents carefully whilst his colleague kept a wary eye on Jameson, he said, "I have been requested to ask you to accompany me to the *Auslandampt*. Don't ask me why, we just had the request over our police radio," and then he smiled a reassuring smile "but I'm sure it can't be serious because we were told 'on no account use force, do so at your peril'."

Jameson was more curious than annoyed as to why he was being asked to go the foreign department. He knew his grade rank of field operator would be sufficient to pull him out of any jam he might be in, in countries of the Western Bloc or neutrality.

He shrugged one shoulder and said, "Jump in and let's not keep the Foreign Office waiting." The foreign department it appeared was housed in the imposing Police Headquarters building at the border town with Germany, Salzburg. Salzburg was famous for it's pastries and coffee shops, narrow streets and fine architectural buildings, and its strict attention to custom. They drove along the cobbled streets, these were sparsely populated by men many of whom wore green waistcoats and Tyrolean hats adorned with long feathers, and women who wore pretty dirndl dresses. He was escorted to the second floor of the main police building by a plain clothes police inspector who had taken over from the uniformed patrolman. The man knocked at the door, hesitated, and entered the room. There were two people in the room drinking coffee and smoking cigarettes, a man and a woman. There was something very familiar about the girl with her back to Jameson. The man spoke in careful English, whilst extending his hand.

"I am Colonel Brauner of Austrian Intelligence and I believe you know Leanna Erhardt."

Jameson shook the proffered hand.

"Of course," he said and went over to her and brushed his lips briefly on her cheek in the fashion of Continentals. "But Leanna you look so different! And you do pop up in the strangest of places at the strangest of times."

She now had short blonde hair and was much slimmer than when Jameson had last seen her, giving the appearance of greater height. To add to the effect she wore an enormous pair of slightly tinted rounded glasses. Spies disguise!

Jameson had worked with her when she had been playing an undercover role for West German Intelligence. After they had smashed the spy-net she had been sentenced to one year's imprisonment in order to preserve her cover, but of course she had not served it. Therefore, he could see the need for a change of appearance, but what was she doing here and more to the point, what was he doing here? Colonel Brauner supplied an answer when he spoke again.

"You see, Mr Jameson, here in Austria we are neutral and so we don't take sides. However, as the head of my Intelligence I have to do what I think is right. I am advised of the normal movements of agents when it concerns me. Just as a matter of courtesy, your Commander Burt's office automatically informed me that you would be coming here. I began to think that I could perhaps do nothing or maybe be of help, but maybe I would have a very delicate situation on my hands. Austria, as I said, is neutral but on four borders we are joining with East and West. Therefore, I have to be careful about incidents. We get intelligence reports about what both sides of the curtain are doing and, of course, we have to be," he spread his hands, "here, so discreet. That Hitler bastard was, after all, originally Austrian and now we're neutral! It has been very good for our economy."

Here he spread his hands again.

"So we have a very close co-operation with our German neighbours, as they are our gateway to the West. And when that signal said that you were on this job I thought it was a good time to contact somebody who would know you. My German friends told me that Leanna here was having a one year 'holiday'." He turned to Jameson and with a wicked expression said in German, "They are so tight those Krauts! And so they pulled Leanna away from her holiday for this job."

Jameson now said his first words having listened to the Colonel's explanation with interest.

"But I thought my job was quite open and shut. I go in, get Coggin, and either I persuade him to give me what I want here, or else I take him back with me, covertly."

Colonel Brauner leaned forward. "Mr Jameson," he said, "you may not believe that I was against the Nazis, because every German or Austrian says that, but because I genuinely was, I was given this top intelligence job. I now have the very difficult job of sitting on the fence! Get Coggin, you can with my blessing, but I cannot officially allow any scandal. Do you understand my position?"

Jameson looked at the man. He was frank. What he was saying was, 'personally I hope you crucify the obnoxious bastard. But don't let me catch you doing anything wrong because if I do, I might have to take a very different attitude if I'm pressured too hard from the other side.' OK. He knew the rules.

Leanna gave the Colonel a grimace to break the awkward silence which developed and said, "Come on, it's not so bad a cooperation we have – is it?"

"Yes, of course, my dear, I'm just giving myself a chance to run away from what I don't see, or something like that." He eyed Jameson sternly, "Be very careful what you do in Austria," he said, and afterwards, "this number I will always be reached at, whatever the time. Strictly emergencies."

He handed a piece of paper containing a telephone number with what were to Peter Jameson unusual digits and then, as if to signify the end of the subject, "But I'm a very bad host, Mr Jameson. Will you have some coffee? And some Cognac with it, perhaps? And then I'll show you both to your hotel room."

*

Leanna Erhardt closed the hotel-room door behind them and looked over her large round spectacles at Jameson who stood in the middle of the room. She pouted her lips and said in a petulant voice:

"Tell me Mr Jameson, why haven't you called me in all these months? And why do we only meet under these circumstances?"

Jameson took up the challenge. He knew very well that she wanted to be with him in that room in Salzburg. She was that sort of a girl. She would not do anything she did not want to do but would be prepared to do a lot for something she wanted.

"Very well Leanna, or Ameli," he said evenly, "I'll get another room. After all, I have got my reputation to think of."

"Leanna for this job," she said, "but still the same Ameli you knew and loved. And no, no, no, no," she continued, "you stay here with me."

He looked at her very closely and then gave the knowing smile he was famous for, "I thought so," he said as he pulled the blonde wig from her head. Her long blonde hair was packed tightly in a small pyramid beneath it. He ran his hands appraisingly over the contours of her body and he pulled a face. "Go and take that corset off," he said gently, "it must feel like a straitjacket."

"You don't change do you?" she said uncomplainingly. "Meet a girl and within five minutes you're telling her to get her clothes off."

"I do change," was his reply. "These days I help 'em."

They stood facing each other in the centre of the traditionally furnished Tyrolean hotel bedroom, their eyes meeting in an understanding of the special chemistry which exists between man and woman when they are of one mind.

Leanna Erhardt had a healthy German girl's sexual urge which she now found being stimulated merely by the exchange of glances. She felt her pulse quickening as her arms reached out for his and they closed in a tight embrace.

Forcing her abdomen against his, her tummy began to tingle with anticipation as difficult to explain things were happening to her. She felt his hands exploring her back with light circular movements. They kissed long and passionately and she felt his fingers nimbly undoing the hook and eye which secured her dress at the base of her neck. She barely felt the zip slide down her back until suddenly his hands were caressing her neatly rounded bottom. He was driving her crazy. His hands were everywhere, stroking, pinching and pressing. She eased her back to help him to undo the last hook of the black one piece corset she wore under her dress and then whispered in his ear, "Come, darling. Let's get rid of these clothes before I go mad!"

"What clothes?" he answered in the barest whisper, removing her dress, corset, panties and stockings in almost one movement. He stared at her momentarily as she stood naked, waiting, then he kissed her large, petulantly jutting breasts in a smother of minute movements.

"My God Leanna. I'd forgotten just how much you turn me on."

It was an ecstatic reunion for both of them, but Jameson chose the time to pose the question that had been nagging in his brain. The cathedral clock chimes for four o'clock were just dying away when he said to her, "OK Leanna. Tell me the real reason why your lot are interested in Coggin. 'Cos I didn't buy the Colonel's story on your presence here for one minute!"

"No, I didn't think it would satisfy you, there's only one thing that does!" she said impudently. "But we had to think of something to say to the Austrians. One of the Russian defectors at Radio Liberty in Munich which, you know having worked for them, is financed by the CIA, turned out not to be a defector at all but a Russian agent who'd been cleverly planted."

"How fiendishly cunning of them!" intoned Jameson. "What next? How did he get caught?"

"Not he, she! Oh not in the usual way, camera in hand photographing the nation's secrets. But even I don't know the exact details. Our Secret Service believes the more secretive the Secret Service is, the more secrets are kept secret, you see," she said smiling.

"But what did she know about Coggin?" asked Jameson.

"You know, I was told not to talk to you about this until we'd actually arrived in Vienna."

"Why?"

"Because according to our Russian, Mark Coggin is working for the CIA."

"Wh-at. I don't believe it. Are you absolutely sure?" he asked incredulously.

"Well, how else would our Russian know? Unless they're feeding phoney bullshit!" She replied and went on. "All this only happened yesterday, so when the Austrians contacted us asking for routine assistance, it just seemed too much of a coincidence."

"You can say that again. I'll still need a lot of convincing that he's a CIA man, unless..." he paused thoughtfully, "the arms racket could be his own idea or more probably, the Russians', as I hardly think even the CIA would finance bombings in London. But the Russians might know an American who would."

"And he is operating on both sides of the curtain?" she queried.

Jameson said, "It certainly would explain a lot of things, wouldn't it? There's one thing that's certain."

"What's that?"

"Now that the Russians know he's a 'double' they'll be very anxious to lay their hands on Mr Coggin. There is quite a queue forming!"

"That," said Leanna Erhardt, "is what I'm supposed to do in Vienna. Put the finger on him, and let them take care of the situation."

"What's happening to Secure-a-World cooperation?"

"It's finding its feet, darling, with our help." Replied Erhardt.

"But we want him back," replied Jameson.

"Which is why," she said, "I wasn't supposed to talk to you until after I'd made my move in Vienna."

"Come on," he said with a smile, "let's sleep on it. What is left of the night to sleep on," and he reached out and snapped off the light. Within minutes they were both sleeping soundly.

The next day dawned cool but crisp, and they packed speedily and drove to the main autobahn from Salzburg to Vienna. The road spanned out in front of them rather like a gigantic snake, winding between the mountainous regions of the country, as if it was unsympathetic to any person trying to penetrate its regions. By means of modern technology the road was wide and good but by necessity it had to wind around the natural terrain of the country, still, progress was fast. Jameson did not drive the Audi to the limit around the mountainous passes but was content to keep the speed of the car to a good average.

Leanna said barely a word but smoked cigarettes and fiddled with the radio which continually faded. Jameson's thoughts were kept within himself. Why did he do this? Why did he allow Commander Burt to put him into this situation? Was it money? Ego? No, not really.

"It's because," he said to himself, "I just kinda' like doing it and I believe in the reasons behind the things I'm doing and lastly, but mostly, because I've got very little choice!"

He shifted the gear of the car one lower as they began to climb a gradually ascending mountain pass. The enormous curve of the road revealed the engineering skills of those Austrian road builders. They had managed to swathe the auto route around the extremities of one of Europe's most mountainous regions. He cautiously noted the signs which said 'beware of rockfall'. A slight movement higher up above the road could be the cause of a shower of rubble and sometimes quite large boulders could descend upon unsuspecting motorists below. They drove in further silence until they cleared the Innsbruck region, she was only preoccupied with her radio fiddling which seemed to him to produce only a succession of yodelling singers, and he with his thoughts and his driving. There was almost no traffic on the road but frequently he had to slow the car to walking pace while small herds of goats scattered and disappeared over, or up, a mountain ridge. His preoccupation with driving and the extreme beauty of the scenery had kept him quiet for such a long time that eventually Leanna Erhardt handed him a lighted cigarette, curled her legs underneath herself on her seat, swivelled round towards him and said: "Really, you're not much fun at all. Five sentences in eighty kilometres! And last night I couldn't stop you talking!"

"Leanna, my lovely, there's time for talking and there's time for thinking, and I've just been doing my thinking that's all!"

He took the cigarette from her and exhaled the smoke in one long steady stream.

"But now I've stopped thinking. What would you say if I suggested that we stop at the next attractive *Gasthaus* and have a *Schoppen* and something to eat?"

She placed her extended fingers on his thigh lightly saying:

"As you say in England, 'what a bloody good idea'!"

Chapter 10
Intrusion Vienna

Vienna, city of intrigue, of the famous old cathedral, of the opulent palace, custodian of Brown's Hotel where most afternoons fashionable people are to be found eating chocolate cake-drinking coffee, and exchanging gossip. It also has on its outskirts the 'Gruen' wine area, which is a collection of exclusive wine gardens, and Vienna's permanent fairground houses the largest Ferris wheel in the world. From it, a visitor may view Vienna in its entirety, and clearly watch the famous Danube river wind its lazy way through the city's heart at the start of its long journey westwards.

Mark Coggin was a patron at Brown's and he was feeling reasonably satisfied with himself at the turn of events, as he sipped his coffee and nibbled the chocolate cake.

There had been nasty moments for him in Yorkshire, but it seemed to him that they were now over, as his telephone call to London had indicated, 'business as usual' with no complications.

He reasoned that it was wise of HH to leave him to travel independently by train, but he could have chosen a more civil method of informing him. This line of thought set him wondering as to the true identity of the mysterious multi-millionaire, who appeared and disappeared at will, and who had openly boasted to him for the first time in Yorkshire of the full extent of his worldwide activities.

It then began to occur to Mark Coggin once again that he knew too much about HH, without knowing who the man really was, for his own good. He, Coggin, was the man who could be exposed to both sides of the curtain, to take all the flack. He pondered over the events of the last few days and began to get the beginnings of an idea for that insurance policy he desired for himself. Other events were about to take a hand in this.

A shadow reflected on his table. He turned round to see that a tall man had appeared at his table.

The man had short, close-cropped, grey hair, and wore a fawn double-breasted, belted raincoat. He had not heard the man approach. The man kept both hands in his raincoat pockets as he spoke to Coggin in Russian.

"Good afternoon, Comrade Coggin, we were expecting you in Prague yesterday."

This was true because HH had appeared briefly in Vienna, but after HH had left Vienna on another mysterious route back to America, Coggin had been approached by the hotel room service waiter who delivered a sealed envelope. It simply contained one sheet of grey note-paper with the scrawled words 'Come immediately to Prague, you know the address'. There had been no signature and Coggin had not replied. Coggin answered the man in Russian also.

"Are you mad? Why do you come here like this? I was planning to leave for Prague in the morning! I got your note." He lied as he had no intention of visiting that capital without certain reassurances from London which he had yet to instigate as part of the Coggin Insurance Policy. The man seated himself unasked at Coggin's table, but still he kept his hands in the raincoat pockets.

"You need not worry, my friend, about me being seen with you. I am unknown outside Czechoslovakia. This is my first visit West. But you are to return with us."

"Us?" queried Coggin.

"Yes. I have a colleague outside with a car. So just pay your bill and leave with me quietly."

"Who are you? I don't know you."

"You will find there have been some changes in the party when you get to Prague," the man replied. "And my name is Boris Gergoff, as you ask. Now shall we go?"

It was hardly an invitation and Coggin looked long and hard at the Russian, then at the bulging raincoat pocket, before signalling the waiter for the bill. They left quietly and without any fuss through the sedate olde-worlde sitting room of Brown's Hotel and through the lobby, which at this late hour of the afternoon was buzzing with activity. It could almost have been a scene from an old-fashioned movie with Mark Coggin as the one being ushered reluctantly out at unseen gun point with only an anxious celluloid audience knowing the truth. However, the reality for Mark Coggin was that between Brown's Hotel and Prague he needed a miracle.

Chapter 11
Uneasy Action

Jameson drove the blue Audi carefully through the old part of Vienna. He could never remember that city's unusual one-way traffic system, but he did remember from his last visit to the city the problem he'd had attempting to cut across the palace forecourt having missed a small turning in the road, inadequately signposted for Brown's Hotel. However, this time he made no mistake and approached Brown's to park behind a green Mercedes waiting at the kerb outside the hotel. Jameson noted the car's Prague registration number plate. As he drew on the handbrake of his car the swing doors to the hotel opened and Mark Coggin appeared followed closely, very closely, by a raincoated man whose right hand was firmly in its pocket.

Peter Jameson took in the scene. Alarm bells rang in his head, he'd seen this kind of thing on film frequently, but happening in real life it somehow seemed different. Coggin was being abducted. Very clearly, without taking his eyes off the scene, but with his mind focused and razor sharp, he said:

"Leanna, you see the guy on the steps, the tall one? That's Coggin, and the guy behind him, coming down the steps with his hand in his pocket, is I think forcibly trying to take him out of Austria – which does not suit our purpose at all. You got a gun?"

She nodded and took out a tiny pistol from the bag she'd kept beneath her seat since they'd left Salzburg.

"OK," he said, "can you take care of the driver of that car in front while I get matey up there? He'll find it difficult to get out 'cos I've parked close to him and boxed him in a treat."

"Yes, I'm ready."

"OK then. Now!"

He opened the door and started to run up the steps. Coggin recognised him and reacted. He jumped backwards, trying to move back into the hotel, and in doing so bumped heavily into the gunman who followed closely behind him. The man tried unsuccessfully to draw the gun from his pocket. In the confusion he pulled the trigger. Jameson, with only a split second to think, dived sideways as he saw what was happening, and was lucky he chose to dive the right way, as the bullet tore furiously through the man's raincoat pocket, ricocheted and whined harmlessly off the stone step, then thudded into the side of the Audi. Meanwhile Leanna Erhardt who was racing towards the Mercedes to tackle the driver was momentarily taken aback by the shooting and half started towards the activity on the steps, but then returned to the car, as the gunman, seeking his opportunity to escape, raced for the vehicle. Coggin's reaction to this change in his fortunes was fast as he disappeared back into the hotel. Jameson, after he'd rolled over avoiding the one shot Coggin's captor had fired at him, retained his grip on the automatic service revolver in his hand, and now aimed carefully. However, by that time the fleeing man was plunging into the passenger seat of the Mercedes. Leanna Erhardt was thrown backwards as the driver of the Mercedes banged the car into reverse at full revs and smashed into the parked Audi, the heavy impact from the Mercedes sending it several feet backwards. The driver shifted the Mercedes into forward gear and as it roared off at high speed, Jameson, still lying on the steps aiming his automatic, squeezed off three shots. The first hit the rear door of the car, the second shattered the passenger seat window and the third missed completely, as the Mercedes sped from sight. The whole scene had been enacted with such speed that bystanders were still standing frozen as Jameson picked himself up and began dusting himself down.

"Are you alright?" Leanna Erhardt asked.

"Yeah," he growled, "we made a right mess of that! What happened to you and the driver? Oh, hang on, here come the cops," as klaxons began to scream.

"I didn't have time to get to him. The shooting started before I could get to his car. And then I wasn't going to risk you putting a bullet through my head," she said, adding hastily, "by mistake, and I couldn't follow them as our car..."

Jameson had already replaced his pistol in its holster as the police now arrived. But they dutifully did as bidden, and raised their hands, as the police approached them, guns drawn; Jameson said to them in German:

"If you feel in my right hand trouser pocket you will find an identification card and one of your security passes duly authorised by your head of security which will explain all this."

One policeman did as asked and Jameson said to him:

"I suggest for the sake of all these gawping bystanders we go along to your police station and verify things there."

The man took a careful look at the ID card and at the telephone number the Austrian Security Chief had written upon the piece of paper Jameson carried in the cover of his security warrant. It contained the very special code. This convinced him of the authenticity of Jameson's ID.

"OK. What happened?"

Jameson explained briefly to the policeman what had happened.

"Did you hit anybody?" he was asked.

"I may have. One round went into the car for sure. Let us see if we can find out what's happened to Coggin – that's his name, the one who got away. He's wanted in England for all kinds of things including in connection with the murder of a policeman. Those words inspired some urgency in the Austrian. He accepted Jameson's authority.

"He dashed back into the hotel, as I said, when he saw me, which is what started the shooting."

They approached the desk clerk who shook his head upon being asked if he had seen the man they described.

"No gentlemen, when I heard the shots I looked through the window beside the door and I see this gentleman shooting at the car and then I get down behind the desk. What are those men, bank robbers or something?"

"Something like that," replied Jameson and, turning to the uniformed policeman, he said, "let's have a quick look round. Although my guess is that he went straight through the hotel and out of any one of the many side doors."

On an impulse Jameson checked the board where the porters hang the room keys. Coggin's room number he had been told was 113. The key to 113 was missing. Another policeman appeared at that moment.

"Come on," Jameson said, "he may be in his room, we'll check it out." He made towards the lift, then said, "We'll use the stairs, but will one of you wait by the lift for a few minutes to make sure he doesn't come down in it. Give us time to get to the first floor and then come up, but carefully mind! Make sure you don't burst in on anything."

Cautiously they made their way to the first floor and approached room 113. They drew their weapons.

They key was in the doorlock so Jameson motioned the policeman to one side of the door, stationed himself to the other side and rapped loudly upon the door with the knuckles of his left hand. The door started to open after a few seconds and Jameson assisted it with a hefty kick with his left leg. There was a startled gasp as the door met the obstruction and flew open wide, knocking violently to the floor the woman who looked to be and was a hotel chambermaid! Jameson did not go immediately to her aid, despite the fact that she lay there looking terrified, in view of the possibility of an obvious trick. He ran his eyes round the room, it seemed empty. He peered through the widening crack in the door jam, at the remaining space behind the door. It was empty. Swiftly he crossed the room to the bathroom and repeated the process. Empty.

The Austrian policeman was kneeling over the *zimmer madchen*, who was not very young and was indeed very shocked.

"Mein Gott," she muttered. *"Mein Gott."*

"I am very sorry madam," the Austrian law officer said, trying hard to keep the smile, which the woman could not see on his face, out of his voice, "but we are looking for a very dangerous criminal and our information was that he was here."

Jameson realised how funny it must have looked to the Austrian policeman from the doorway behind him. Like a Laurel & Hardy film. The woman was struggling to her feet.

"There was a man here," she said, "he left about five minutes ago by the back staircase to the right, I saw him," and she motioned with an outstretched arm.

Mark Coggin was a cool customer, Jameson thought. He must have come straight up to his room, packed his bags and left. They walked the length of the corridor to the window overlooking the street on to which the back staircase exit led. It was thronged with people on their way home from work. It was hopeless. Coggin had got clean away.

They returned for the policeman to take a statement from the chambermaid and Jameson rejoined the others, who were waiting at the entrance to Brown's Hotel.

He explained to Leanna Erhardt what had happened. She looked at him and said:

"In the words of the English, the bird has flown."

He nodded unhappily. "Yeah, we're not exactly getting the breaks the good guys are supposed to get here, are we?"

He shrugged his shoulders. "OK, let's get down to police headquarters where we can at least do a little private planning!"

On the way he surveyed the caved-in front of the Audi, and said ruefully, "We'll need to get another car. This one's had it." He whispered to her, "I think with your charm you could do that for us while I ride with the man in charge here, and

Leanna," he whispered again to her, "either undo another button and show 'em the whole lot (which might help charm a new set of wheels for us) or do the one up that insists on popping open!"

Only her eyes moved to look below her shoulders and she casually brought them back to look him straight between the eyes, and with a syrupy smile on her lips she said mockingly:

"Peter Jameson, I do declare you are the biggest bastard I have ever seen and I wish that gunman had put a bullet down your horrible sarcastic throat." This in a passable southern American drawl.

But to the onlooker out of earshot she could have been saying anything. Who knows what who says?

It was beginning to snow as they left the police station and were driving to their hotel. Jameson had listened to the mild rebuke which had reverberated over the amplified telephone of the officer in charge of the main police station in Vienna. It had come from Colonel Brauner in Salzburg. Jameson knew it was an act that the Colonel needed to go through for the benefit of his colleagues in Vienna and accepted it. It had not helped that a message had come in, before the Colonel had finished. There'd been a pause and then Colonel Brauner had said:

"Mr Jameson. It seems your second shot was either lucky or remarkably accurate, because we have just found the man Boris Gergoff shot through the head, just four miles from our border with Czechoslovakia. You will not know the name but it is the man who tried to shoot you and then escaped."

Peter Jameson was tired as they left police headquarters in the car the Austrians (Erhardt's charm having succeeded) had loaned him and he pulled the windscreen-wiper switch to double speed to increase his vision as the snow flurries increased. When it snowed under the right circumstances the surroundings looked really pretty. He was well-equipped as he'd bought the leather jacket he'd selected on the plane into Zurich, together with the most expensive accessories, and the shop had not been in any way surprised when he'd asked them to parcel up his English clothes and send them back to Knightsbridge.

"No trouble, of course, sir. And no charge whatsoever," they'd said, "all part of the service."

He appreciated the warm boots now.

Leanna was leaning against him. She felt she should say something but when she did it came as a surprise to him under the circumstances.

"I wonder what you were like before you were in this business?" she said. "Because I just happened to look at you when they said they'd found the man dead. You showed no emotion at all, but you killed him. It was your bullet..."

"Wrong," he interrupted before she could go further, "A field agent has no place to be thinking such thoughts. About the emotion, first of all I didn't choose this job, I was..." he wondered if he should go further, but continued, "I was pushed into it, and trained to do it, and then that man fired at me first. It could be me on the slab."

"Could you have killed him in cold blood?"

"Oh yes, I tried to and if I had, by now we'd have Coggin."

They were approaching Brown's and the subject was changed.

"If this snow keeps up overnight we won't recognise this nice new car in the morning."

He left the keys with the porter, and went to reception for the room key.

"Upstairs, sir," said the clerk.

"Thanks," he said and they made for the lift.

Wearily Leanna turned the key and they entered the room. The light snapped on and Coggin's voice greeted them from an armchair in the room.

"Hallo, sunshine! I thought it was time you and I did some talking. And tell me, who's the little lady?"

"Hallo, Coggin," replied Jameson calmly (pretending to be cool was the best policy), as if it were an everyday occurrence to walk into your hotel room with nothing but sleep on your mind and to find the very man the entire Austrian police force is seeking, sitting in your armchair with a gun in his hand.

Coggin said, "Now if we're not going to have any heroics from either of you, you can sit down and listen to what I've got to say. And join me in a drink?"

On the table stood a bottle of Grants Standfast and some glasses.

"Don't try any of that hairy old nonsense of throwing whisky in my face because it doesn't work and I'd have to shoot you. Then you wouldn't hear what I've got to say. And it would waste damned good whisky."

Jameson chuckled to himself. What Coggin did not realise was that the Beretta he held in his right fist was useless as Jameson had removed the firing pin from it on that Yorkshire-bound train, and therefore he might just as well be pointing a water pistol at them.

"Who are you madam? And where do you fit in?" asked Coggin, glancing towards Leanna.

"I am Leanna Erhardt. Where do I fit in? I work for West German Intelligence. It is not important to keep that secret from you."

Coggin chuckled, "West German Intelligence, eh! Well this is all very cosy. I work for the CIA and the Russians." He turned to Jameson. "You don't seem surprised. I presume you work for the British?"

"Special Branch. And no I'm not surprised."

"I see. I began to wonder about you some time ago. You kept popping up in too many places, and when you came charging up the hotel steps like Al Capone, my suspicions were justified. You did me a big big favour though – but I'll tell you about that with the rest of my proposition. Have that drink and sit down."

"Shall I get them?" asked Leanna. Coggin nodded and sat down.

"You realise, of course," Jameson said, "that every policeman in Vienna is looking for you, including me, so what you've got to say had better be good!"

"Look, sunshine. I've been in this business a long time. A lot longer than you I suspect, and I know the kind of deals that can be cut. Sometimes the most unlikely ones. And that's what I'm after – a deal."

"OK. What've you got to offer?"

"Oh no, not that easy. First of all you couldn't make my kind of deal but I think your boss could. Who is he?"

"I can contact him easily enough when I think it necessary," said Jameson. "But I have more authority than you think."

He crossed his feet suddenly, testing, and Coggin jerked the Beretta from his lap in Jameson's direction.

"Take it easy for God's sake, Coggin, do you want to wake up the whole hotel?

"Just don't try anything, that's all," said Coggin.

"You're much too nervous!"

Leanna finished her Scotch and reached over for a refill. Jameson turned towards her.

"Leanna," he said, "better pour Mr Coggin a large one. His nerves are shot to pieces! Now then, sunshine", he spat the words sarcastically, "as they say in 'B' movies. Talk."

Mark Coggin cleared his throat, took a long draught of his whisky and began.

"I'll presume for the sake of simplicity that you don't know too much about me." If he expected a reply from Jameson, he got none.

"By force of circumstance, financial, not political, and the way things have turned out, I am working for both sides. The Americans recruited and trained me many years ago and left me as a 'sleeper' until needed. They backed my legitimate business to further my cover and it also suited them in awkward times to have my company sell some arms, say to South Africa or awkward Arab countries like Iraq, when it would have been embarrassing, or even impossible, for a US firm to do this."

Peter Jameson looked across to Leanna Erhardt who'd opened her mouth to say something and said to her, "Let him finish Leanna. I've heard weirder stories."

Coggin continued. "The Russians found out about me. This wasn't difficult. And for the lure of money, and prominence on the other side of the curtain, I agreed. I'm quite an important person in Czechoslovakia you know."

Jameson could not resist saying, "Yeah, I noticed. You must also be very popular with the relatives of those your explosives have killed in Ireland, and the UK."

Coggin replied, "Look, sunshine." How Jameson was beginning to hate that expression. "In this business you have to recognise there will be casualties. People don't care if a few thousand Koreans or Chinese or Vietnamese get chopped, but they kick up a hell of a fuss when it's close to home. It's all relative you see."

"You don't convince me as easily as you've convinced yourself. But then you just want to justify actions which have been motivated firstly by greed and secondly by power. But go on. How do you justify all those blackmail victims?" Jameson shot at him.

Coggin looked startled, "You know more than I thought."

"Oh," Jameson said.

He'd have to be careful not to fall into this trap of exchanging rhetoric with Coggin again, so he explained hastily, "A Minister came under the surveillance of our firm when he was discovered to be using the services of a special call girl, a standard check-up," he said, trying to be as convincing as he could. "But go on."

"Got it!" Coggin reflected. "So that's why you were going to the Fanlight Club and I helped you with a bump," he chuckled, "and here we are."

"Not too long ago," continued Coggin, "I was called to a meeting in the States with three high-ranking officers of the CIA. At first I thought I'd been rumbled and my first reaction was not to go. But then I reasoned that if that were so I'd have been quietly bumped off elsewhere, not called to a special meeting in the States. There I found that they were trying to put the finger on a character who seemed to be a very wealthy person in the US and who, through his wealth, was wielding great political power. One of the things they couldn't find out was the identity of this person, there was such an undergrowth of nominees and companies, not just in the US, that this person remained a complete mystery. The person was known only as HH and had international conglomerates. They thought he might be behind arms sales in a big way, and that's why they thought it was time to activate me, they thought I was the perfect agent for their purposes. They suspected that even the President of the US might not be exactly 'blameless'."

Jameson was now becoming very interested as Coggin went on.

"Well, sunshine. I know the identity of this man, and I also know what he is doing to the British…" he paused and chose his words carefully, "to the very heart of the British Government. And that's what I've got to bargain with. Pretty big stuff."

Jameson was learning rapidly, just how vital the use of tactics is in espionage, as a good cricketer learns them to be essential in the game of cricket. Coggin, Jameson figured, could only guess at how much he knew and get more worried, which could lead him to slip up – and cock up! But he did not delude himself, he was tackling a very powerful organisation in which Coggin was only a snaky middle man. It was HH & Co Jameson needed to nail, and maybe half of Ireland! But Coggin was his route to him, providing his tactical game was good. And he did have Anna Dubric working undercover. His problem with her was her communication with him. He would need to send her a fax giving the open plan drop.

Jameson spoke. "You can put the gun away," he said quietly. "I've heard enough. But I'm gonna find it difficult to get you an answer just like that. I can hardly phone what you've just told me. You haven't given me any facts. You'll have to tell me more. You say you know who HH is, so tell me, who is he?"

Coggin shook his head, "No more yet, sunshine. Get serious will you? You will know just enough for you to find a way to arrange a meeting with your boss, and that's all."

Jameson knew that before he could get any kind of deal from Commander Burt, he would have to get at least some evidence. He knew Coggin had something very important to say, but then he'd had the benefit of the situation build up. Chair-bound government planners could only guess at the facts and relied on their field agents to act and support their actions with evidence for the records, however manufactured. He said to Leanna Erhardt:

"Why don't you go to bed," and he looked at Coggin, "and I'll drink with you down to where it says 'Standfast' on the label." He nodded towards the bottle on the table.

"You should know, sunshine, that when I drink, I drink," and his eyes found the girl's. "Don't worry about me, I'll sleep on this sofa like a baby. Just keep some space in your bed next door for sunshine here," a nod came in Peter Jameson's direction.

She rose to her feet, as Jameson tipped some of the amber liquid into the two remaining glasses.

"I am tired, and I can take a hint," she said and left the sitting room to disappear into the bedroom.

Jameson turned to Coggin after the door had closed.

"Let's forget that we don't like each other," he said raising his glass.

"Nonsense," was the reply. "I like you. But you were a considerable threat to me that's all, and now, I think you are going to be a considerable ally."

"OK. You can start by telling me who killed Fisher!"

"That was an accident. But it wasn't me. Oh! So that's how you got on to me. He had passed on information."

Jameson nodded. Better to let Coggin think that than to compromise Anna.

"He got a message to me," he lied.

The words 'Standfast' had been reached on the bottle by the time Jameson had persuaded Coggin to give him some sketchy details of the financial speculation that had been revealed by HH in Bradford before Fisher's death had brought about the dramatic turn of events. Fisher had not died in vain. He had caused Coggin to run and now, surreptitiously, Jameson gleaned from Coggin how HH had been consistently devaluing the British pound and in so doing making immense amounts of money for himself. The treasury and intelligence units would piece together this information on receipt of Coggin's documents. It would be the turn of certain officials in the Treasury to get the hard look that strikes terror in the hearts of even innocent men when security moves in. Yes, Commander Burt would certainly take action. Jameson went to the bedroom with a singing but satisfied head. He was very pleased with the session. His headache was all in the cause of duty, or should he just tell that to the Alka Seltzers in the morning! He was excited at his news but upon entering the bedroom he saw that Leanna was fast asleep, lying face downwards. 'How typical of a woman,' he thought. 'Just close the eyes and crash. Don't bother about what is going on in the next room. Could this be the difference between the sexes?'

Jameson turned around. Already Coggin had curled his feet under him on the sofa and his eyes were closed. He was beginning to breathe evenly and slowly. He must feel secure, thought Jameson, as he closed the door, but he took no chance and turned the key in the lock.

From his 'Q' kit he took a piece of equipment known in the trade as 'Swiss Board'. This is a highly explosive material which has the appearance of a thin slice of processed cheese. One full slice of it looks as though it would make a tasty 'Kraft Cheese' sandwich, but the material in Jameson's hand only required battery detonation to explode the device causing damage to the door and to the person trying to open the door. As Jameson tore a small strip from the Swiss Board and connected it between the key in the door using his battery operated cigarette lighter as a power unit, he grimly reflected what might happen if there was somebody you really wanted to 'get', about to take a bite out of a carefully prepared sandwich, when someone turned a certain transmitter to the allotted waveband. A somewhat long distance toothache! It must be time to join Leanna's tousled head on the pillow, if he was thinking things like that, he told himself. Nothing would happen unless somebody from the other side of his door inserted metal into the keyhole in the door and touched the key. If this happened there would be a small explosion which would blow a hole in the door and discourage whoever was attempting to get in, Jameson surmised, and in the process would certainly wake him up. He could now sleep unafraid of surprises. He climbed into the bed beside Leanna as she slept on peacefully.

Leanna woke him in the morning with customary overtures and pointing a finger at the curious contraption he'd rigged up the previous night said:

"What on earth...?"

He briefly explained what had transpired. She listened attentively and then said again with womanly directness:

"I don't like Mark Coggin, don't you think to even try to deal with him is a mistake!"

"A mistake," chided Jameson, "is something you have made, not something you are about to make."

She made a face at him. "Don't you start on me with your BBC English."

"Oh come on, Leanna, you know what I mean. I want not only to get him and to discredit the Russians, but also to uncover this mysterious HH. And I think, if I play our cards right, we'll do just that. Now will you go along with that? Or do I send you home?"

"I can't refuse you because we're involved now, so there's your answer."

He looked at her silently for a brief moment.

"OK," he said, extending the little finger of his left hand. "A deal. We'll get 'em all together, but carefully."

"OK," she said. "So we need a plan. Have you got one?"

He nodded. "But I will tell you exactly what we know, and when I say we, I mean the British and me, because I learned a lot last night, drinking Scotch with Mark Coggin. And I've yet to decide how much of what I learned I should share with London. And by the way, I don't think I could have done anything except break Coggin's neck, if I'd found out he'd had anything to do with Fisher's death."

He spoke rapidly to Leanna, explaining the circumstances. She nodded perfunctorily, from time to time posing a brief question. When he'd finished she said:

"That's quite a story. Now what do you have in mind?"

He answered her clearly, outlining the facts.

"First of all, like you I don't trust Coggin one inch, not one centimetre. So we've got to watch him. We'll need to protect him. This means as far as we can he's got to be to with us. We can't let him use us for his own ends. Let him think he is. And I don't believe he's played all his cards yet. There are also those two Americans in London running the Coggin arms organisation, but we'll have to let Commander Burt's ground forces there take care of them for now. But I have a secret weapon in play on that front."

He was swiftly stowing the previous night's booby trap into his 'Q' briefcase as he talked, and this done he said to Leanna, "Come on, time to wake him up, and then time for me to have a long phone call with London while you keep him occupied."

Chapter 12

Swansong Vienna

Even though Mark Coggin had on a large anorak with its hood pulled well up over his head, as they left the hotel Jameson was feeling somewhat nervous. It was snowing heavily and the sparsely populated streets gave some refuge, few people had any interest in anything other than going about their own business and trying to keep as warm as possible in the bleak, wintry conditions. The trio reached the car and Leanna began to brush the snow from it, with long sweeping movements of her hands which were covered with fox-fur gloves. Jameson's instructions from Commander Burt had been quite explicit. Get Coggin to Switzerland and then he, Burt, would talk about a deal. Coggin had insisted to Peter Jameson on Switzerland and this led Jameson to suspect that after the previous day's events Coggin could be becoming apprehensive about his Eastern image. For Commander Burt to even travel to the neutral country of Switzerland meant that he was more than interested in Coggin, particularly as he'd told Jameson that his visit had to be 'silent' which meant to Jameson, no local help, and he had to get Coggin through while maintaining the status quo; which was all very well but for the fact that Coggin was officially wanted in Austria and Germany and Peter Jameson had therefore to pit his wits against these people in order to ensure the mission's success. Much as he was not looking forward to this awkward journey through the snow he had to admit to himself that the elements were in his favour. Under these conditions officials would not be too diligent, and furthermore they would not be looking for two men and a girl. However, he was not so concerned about official intervention (policemen can be seen and avoided), as he was about Coggin's other enemies.

His thoughts dwelled on these possibilities as he turned the key in the ignition to start the car. It started readily enough but the engine seemed to be running lumpily. He adjusted the choke but it made no difference.

"What's the matter, sunshine?" came Coggin's voice from the back of the official VW.

"It's only running on three," replied Jameson. "I'll have to have a look." He pulled his collar up around his neck, stepped out into the heavy snow and went round to lift the bonnet of the rear-engined car. He saw the fault immediately. The lead from the third spark plug had become disconnected. He snapped the lead connection into place and immediately the motor took on a smoother tone. As he turned around to retrace his steps to the driver's seat, he became aware of a car parked some twenty yards to his rear. It contained two occupants. Its motor was running as was that of the car directly behind it. Under the pretext of wiping the rear window Jameson swiftly took stock of the situation. There were two identical Volkswagens (Beetles, the same as his) and it seemed they had been waiting for him. He lifted the bonnet once more and reached forward to press the button on the specially fitted device on the car's carburettor. This device was a modern super-charger and whilst it played havoc with the vehicle's fuel consumption, it gave it markedly increased acceleration and another 20 mph on top speed (this was an Alpine Corps vehicle). Not all of Austria's unmarked police cars were so equipped, but this vehicle had yet another device which could well prove useful: retractable spikes on its tyres, operated by a lever from inside the car. His activities had not escaped Leanna's attention.

"What's wrong?" She said as he slammed the driver's door after him and put the car into gear.

"A plug lead had jumped loose," he replied innocently.

"So why did you engage the super-charger?" She countered. "I heard the air suction as soon as you did it."

Jameson was watching his two driving mirrors carefully as he drove the car in the direction of the town centre. The first VW was keeping a respectable distance from their car and although Jameson made several manoeuvres which would have caused an innocent motorist to overtake to the accompaniment of a shaken fist and a probable torrent of abuse, this car stayed where it was and reaffirmed Jameson's initial judgement.

"We're being followed," he said.

Leanna Erhardt pulled the sun visor down to use the vanity mirror. Coggin leant forward to study the scene through it.

"I noticed them", Jameson said, "in the car park when I was fixing the plug lead. That's why I put the blower on. They're using two cars."

He caught Coggin's eyes in his driving mirror, "I think it must be your Czech friends. They must want you rather badly, methinks, but I can't see them pulling anything in the town. And," he added, "they are probably very curious about Leanna and me. I think we'll stop and have a coffee and study our route to Geneva very carefully on the map. I've thought of a fantastic little plan but it'll need split second timing and excellent map reading."

"That's me," said Leanna.

"And that leaves me as observer," said Coggin from behind.

"Here, use this," said Leanna and she produced from her leather shoulder bag the sort of mirror travelling girls seem to carry these days, about six inches square with a collapsible stand attached to its back. Jameson drove carefully through the snowy streets of Vienna. He'd formulated a daring plan in his head, but he was not sure just how far to trust Mark Coggin. By his own admission Coggin was working for the Russians and the Americans, he'd also been responsible for countless deaths and inestimable misery for personal gain, through his arms dealing and bombing activities, and furthermore he had spearheaded a blackmailing organisation, the like of which had never before been known in the United Kingdom. But he had not done all of this on his own. He'd had the immense backing of the mysterious HH who, it now seemed certain, had played on both sides of the curtain and had now decided that Coggin knew too much about him and planned either to take him forcibly into the East or to eliminate him. Jameson knew not which but suspected the latter.

Well, Commander Burt needed Coggin's knowledge, so in the short term it had to be Coggin who was with them. He'd be no use to them as a captive in the Eastern Bloc or, at this stage, dead. He swung the car into a convenient parking place by the kerb and said over his shoulder:

"Now keep the hood of your anorak well over your head, Mark. We don't want some keen-eyed young cop getting lucky."

"Don't worry, sunshine."

The trio trouped through the thickly populated town centre until they came to one of the many fashionable coffee houses. They entered, chose a table well away from the window and ordered a large pot of coffee. Leanna Erhardt produced from nowhere a large-scale map of the area and the three of them studied it carefully. The coffee came and Jameson poured it. A strong one for Coggin and weaker ones for Leanna and himself. Very soon the strong coffee had its desired effect on Coggin and he excused himself hurriedly and left the table. This gave Jameson the precise chance he had engineered for a few moments alone with Leanna.

He swiftly told Leanna of his plan and finished by saying, "Now, when I'm not there you'll have to watch Coggin like a hawk. At the moment he's nervous and knows his former Czech friends are after him for his knowledge of their organisation amongst other things, and HH almost certainly ordered that so he's prepared to do a deal with Commander Burt. But he's a double-dealing rat. If we take the heat off him he may just decide he'd be better off to cut and run. After all, he's asking the British to mark his card for him and not to press charges of treason, and he wants money! But my bet is, if he knows what I think he knows about this HH, he'll get his deal from us backed by the American paymasters. This HH seems to have so much influence that, not only does he manipulate politics and big business in the States, he also gets the Russians and their allies to act as his hatchet men. And one last thing, Coggin's gun is useless."

"Useless, how?"

Jameson explained to her how he'd removed its firing pin. She pulled a face, "And I was suffering more from hypertension due to his pointing the thing at me than tiredness when I went to bed last night."

"Well, we don't know yet whether or not it would be better to have him armed or not and it certainly could work against us," said Jameson.

"Hang on, here he comes."

"Sorry about that," said Coggin, returning with a bland smile on his face, "got caught short."

The three of them rehearsed their plan once more and Leanna Erhardt made careful route markings on the map with her pencil.

"You know, Jameson," said Coggin after they'd paid the bill and were leaving the restaurant, "you're a damned good planner and what's more, you've got a cunning mind. You'd make a lot of money if you weren't so straight."

"Who said anything about me being so straight, Mark? I make quite a few bob as it is, and besides, I've not had the right opportunity yet."

This last sentence brought a thoughtful look into Coggin's eyes, and he stayed silent as they retraced their steps to the car. Jameson's practised eye checked to make sure the car had not been interfered with, as he walked around to the driver's door he was pleased to note that the only footsteps, which were now half filled, had belonged to them. One 'bandit' car was parked, he noticed, on the other side of the street and the other 'bandit' was not immediately to be seen but was no doubt somewhere in the immediate vicinity. Charitably, Jameson waited for the traffic to clear in order that his tail would have no difficulty in exercising the U-turn it needed to continue to follow them. This was duly done and they set out in the direction of Innsbruck. To make the plan work successfully, Jameson had calculated that their adversaries would wish to make their attack, on what they believed to be an unsuspecting quarry, in the loneliest possible area, but close to the border of one of the Eastern Bloc countries. Jameson avoided the autobahn, preferring the land-strasse, where conditions were tricky and thus in his favour.

"Mark," he called out, "strapped under your seat is the M16. Will you check it, and load it? In your profession you should know how!"

His eyes enquired of Coggin in the driving mirror. Coggin brought the weapon from under his legs and laid it on his lap.

"Worth £100 each in Russia," was Coggin's reply.

Jameson watched him in his mirror as he checked the bolt action and thrust the first bullet into the breech chamber, and with the automatic rifle still on his lap resumed his observation using Leanna's mirror. They drove in near silence for more than an hour. Jameson had chosen this route because he knew there would be some traffic on it, but not heavy traffic. Coggin spoke, "The second bandit's behind the first one now," he said. "I think they're starting to get restless."

"Yeah, I've seen him. How much further until we turn off, Leanna?" Jameson asked.

Leanna was looking at the map making rapid calculations as Jameson pulled the 'tyre spike' lever and squeezed past a double-trailer truck in front of them, accelerating violently. Here was his chance to make a rapid advance and put some distance between them and their pursuing enemy. With maximum road purchase he would gain ground and their pursuers would be stuck behind that truck, with any luck for three or four kilometres.

"I reckon about nine clicks," she said.

"Nine k's, OK, hold on to your hats, here we go."

He drove with great skill at a speed which could only be described, in the conditions, as highly dangerous, for the next quarter of an hour. His objective was to avoid a confrontation with their enemy until he chose the time and the place. He did not want to lose the element of surprise and to have had a chase for 8 or 9 kms could only have done that.

"OK," said Leanna, "the turn off's just coming up."

He slowed down a little.

"Thanks," he said as he accepted a lighted cigarette from Coggin, "I'll let them catch up enough for them to see where we turn off."

He cruised casually and checked his watch. So far they'd gained about two and a half minutes on their pursuers. Three minutes by the time he saw their lights blazing, about one kilometre behind. Perfect, he thought.

It had now stopped snowing but the dull winter's day gave sparse visibility.

"Turning coming up about 200 metres ahead," said Leanna.

"I see it," replied Jameson "and they can see me."

By now he was crawling and the two pursuing VWs were approaching at a speed which must have been close to 100 kph on the snow-covered road. At the very last moment he signalled a left turn, and made the manoeuvre. By this time bandits one and two, as they had nicknamed them, were less than fifty yards behind and they hopelessly overshot the turning, the rear bandit bumping the skidding first bandit, and pushing him on to the rough verge, on the opposite side of the road.

Jameson now drove in earnest, he was on a rough, B class road and according to their map-reading they had ten kilometres to drive before they reached the lonely wood they had chosen and over this distance Jameson had to gain a least two minutes on his pursuers. He drove the slithering, sliding car almost to the limit, the extra power and traction giving him the confidence he needed to take the risks required to put them in a position to carry out the daring plan. He calculated that when they came to the ambush area he would need between one and one and a half minutes to run the two hundred yards necessary and scramble into a suitable position. But he must be in position before their enemy sighted them. Now they were leaving the wooded area and entering a clearing with more woods beyond it.

"This looks like it, sunshine," said Coggin quietly, "don't stop too close to the edge of those trees."

Jameson drove as close as he dared, then jammed on the brakes, causing the car to slide into the broadside and to come to a halt sideways. He grabbed the rifle from Coggin and with Leanna Erhardt's, "Good luck, Peter, shoot straight," ringing in his ears he ran like hell. It seemed to him that the clearing would never end. 'Had he miscalculated?' There was a natural rise to the left and this was what he made for. He arrived at the fringe of the trees panting from his exertions and ran his eye swiftly around the site looking for the most suitable position. He found the spot he wanted, but had scant time for rehearsal; lying full length, controlling his breathing, splaying his feet and legs into an arch, with his insteps and knees pressing into the ground for support, his legs and body taut, he waited. His hands held the automatic rifle steady with his elbows making the tripod. With his left hand he adjusted the sight of the weapon. He closed one eye and took a swift but careful practice aim. For his and Commander Burt's plan to succeed, there had to be no hostile Czechoslovak witnesses left alive. Those were his orders – to himself – Mark Coggin had to disappear entirely without trace.

He lowered the weapon and waited. Leanna Erhardt and Mark Coggin were out of the car struggling as if to push it. They stopped and looked in his direction and he waved his hand, yes, he was ready. He used the waiting time to examine his plan critically, thinking, could something have gone wrong? Surely they should be here by now! He had already planned his strategy, which relied heavily on surprise and accuracy. It was unlikely they'd approach in a bunch, so he'd shoot from right to left; which was how he'd planned the angle of approach. This would give him his best chance. He reasoned that after the first shot the reaction of the attackers would be to stop and then to try to get back to their vehicles, so if he hit the last one first he could then pick them off as they struggled for safety. Leanna Erhardt and Coggin were to dive behind their car at the sound of his first shot. He saw the flash of the car's lights first of all as they appeared from the darkness of the trees and sped towards the stationary Volkswagen. They decreased their speed as they sighted the stationary car. Jameson flexed his fingers several times before lifting his weapon, pulling it with his left hand and cradling it into his right shoulder. The two cars stopped yards from their quarry and doors flew open even before the cars had stopped and men began running towards their intended victims. Jameson now felt very calm and he took careful aim at the last man, breathed out slowly, then held his breath and squeezed the trigger. The velocity of the bullet as it struck the man and spun him sideways before he fell in a crumpled heap. Jameson pumped three more shots in rapid succession at the now retreating men with deadly accuracy, and then – just as quickly as it had begun – it was all over. Jameson leapt to his feet as the last man fell, and ran as fast as his legs would allow him until he reached the scene where death had struck so violently. Coggin stood by the fallen men. They were all dead. He looked in awe, and then at Jameson:

"Bloody hell, I've never seen anything like it. Incredible, sunshine," this he repeated over and over again. "I didn't have time to even get my bloody gun out."

"We are well-trained in Special Branch," said Jameson quietly, as he struggled to breathe evenly, "I just hope you're worth it. I just hope you're worth it."

His range instructor would have been proud of his shooting; he had struck like an avenging angel. But whilst anyone hearing those shots could conceivably have mistaken them for a hunting party, they would have to remove the carnage now blocking the road. Blood from the dead bodies was staining the snow, making the scene even more gruesome.

"Come on, Mark," Jameson said gruffly, "Let's clear up here."

Leanna Erhardt helped remove the signs of the blood stained ambush by kicking the loose snow where the bodies had fallen, and then scooping fresh snow over the last remaining marks. The corpses were loaded into the two cars and Jameson and Coggin drove the cars and occupants deep into the woods, where they were abandoned. Jameson shivered when they began their more sedate drive towards Switzerland. He'd just killed four men in cold blood. What was it Leanna Erhardt had asked him only last night? Could he kill in cold blood? Well, he just had. Coggin noticed the shiver and produced a hip flask which he handed to Jameson.

"Have a slug of this, sunshine," he said. "If you hadn't killed them, they'd have certainly got us. I congratulate you. A beautiful plan, brilliantly executed. You have the Coggin seal of approval!"

Jameson took the flask to his lips and swiftly jerked his head backward. The fiery liquid tingled at the nape of his neck before producing a warm glow throughout the upper part of his body.

"Thanks," he said and they drove onwards in silence.

Chapter 13
Tension

In the Fanlight Club the atmosphere was, as ever, cosy and intimate. Expensively, revealingly clad hostesses mingled with businessmen, the hard-eyed girls assessing how much money could be prised from their customers, and the men assessing their chances with the girls. Drinks were flowing freely.

"Care to buy me a drink, sir?" asked Anna of Commander Burt.

He had appeared without notice. He sat at the table with her, eyeing her charms as would any other unaccompanied businessman seeking feminine company. His presence gave her cause for some concern. Had something happened to Jameson? What was the cause of his unannounced visit?

"I believe champagne is the drink here?" he said expansively, and signalled to the waitress who appeared quickly at his elbow. She took their drinks order and after she'd disappeared into the darkened bar area, he spoke rapidly to Anna.

"Miss Dubric, Anna, I need some information." She nodded as he went on. "Now listen. We could wind up this whole Coggin operation in England quietly and quickly. Stop the bombings, remove the blackmail victims, but I'm sure all it would achieve would be a lull. A lull before it all started again." He observed her puzzled expression and continued. "You see, I'm not at all certain that Coggin is the top man. His disappearance leads me to think that there's someone else or another nest. Jameson is suggesting he suspects that."

"Is that why you have come to see me Commander," she said. "You could have phoned me?"

"Of course I could. But you know every now and then I do what I used to do quite a lot when I was about thirty years old. If I feel like a night out I go and have a bit of fun following my instincts!"

"You!" she said in disbelief. "I don't believe it."

He picked up the glass which had been placed before him, twiddled it in his fingers and sipped the champagne.

"Tasty stuff, this," he said. "I suppose you drink it like water?"

She leaned towards him revealing her cleavage with the practised skill of a nightclub hostess as she said, "Water, my dear Commander, is for washing in, champagne stimulates the desire for pleasure. But quite a lot gets poured into the potted plant by the Ladies."

"You turn out to be quite the philosopher as well as a passably good undercover lady!" He said. "Now then, tomorrow I am flying to Switzerland to see Jameson and Coggin, that is if Jameson gets him through."

"You mean he's found Mark Coggin?"

"Yes, of course, but he's got some problems over there and he'll need all his resourcefulness to get Coggin from Austria into Switzerland. It's a long story which I don't want to go into here and I've told you enough to enable you to know the direction in which Jameson wants you to dig."

"Well, what do you want from me?"

"First of all a dance, my dear. Don't look so shocked. It won't look out of place here!"

Mike Lopez Riser, who hailed from the south American part of the West Indies, began to sing 'Those eyes are the eyes of a woman in love' as the Commander and Anna Dubric made their way to the tiny dance floor. Commander Burt thought Mrs Commander Burt would have to be very understanding to understand this.

It was easy to talk on the minute dance floor. The club was so designed that the music did not intrude upon the clientele, and as the loudspeakers were strategically placed, it was possible to converse with your partner if that was one's desire, or to just soak up the musical entertainment offered.

Commander Burt said to Anna Dubric, "I want you to think back over the period of your association with Mark Coggin and to try to remember."

"What?" she said directly.

"Well, during the time you have known Coggin has there been any person who has been a friend, a confidant? You know, someone who has been around, not necessarily a lot, but over a long period. I need a lead. Something to bargain with tomorrow. I don't think you're withholding anything, but you might unwittingly know something or somebody who could belong to the scenario. Think!"

It was at that precise moment that Lord Lander entered the club and crossed the dance floor to take up a seat where he would have an unopposed view of the coming striptease acts. Anna stiffened.

"That person who has just walked in front of us and sat down there," she motioned with her hand, "is Lord Lander".

A light began to dawn in Commander Burt's mind. Of course, Lander. His name had been cropping up constantly through this whole affair. Maybe he wasn't just a victim but the one sitting up there with his hereditary peerage in the House of Lords and putting the finger on potential blackmail victims. He should have instigated a closer investigation when the original contacts had revealed the involvement. But it had seemed that Lord Lander's involvement had been no worse than a dozen other highly placed officials; his attraction to the opposite sex was such that he was prepared to pay handsomely for favours in many and often unusual forms.

Commander Burt hummed quietly to himself as he propelled Anna around the dance floor doing a clumsy cross between a 'twist' and a half jive, and she was quite relieved when the fanfare interrupted the dancing for the floorshow. After leading Anna Dubric back to their darkened table, Commander Burt excused himself. He made a rapid phone call on his way to the gentlemen's washroom, and then returned to his table to resume his evening as though he had not a care in the world.

Lord Lander was feeling perky as he prepared to leave the Fanlight Club. He felt light-hearted and his step was jaunty. He'd spoken with Mike Riser about the possibilities of the dusky mannish Jamaican stripper who could contort her body into the most unbelievable positions to perform her act. An imaginary body dance movement, which ended with her lying upon a goatskin rug, and simulating love movements with a toy snake. Money had changed hands, and the girl's address with a key wrapped inside it in Lander's pocket, she would be a perfect foil for Lander's bisexual perversions. He gave the doorman a five pound note and a taxi appeared as if by magic. He stepped into the cab after giving the address he had memorised to the driver, and the black taxi cab rumbled off into the darkness in the direction of nearby Mayfair. It was only then that he realised he was not alone. The interior light of the taxi snapped on to reveal an unsmiling face upon whose head reposed a green trilby hat. The man held the plastic covered blue warrant card between forefinger and thumb.

"Special Branch, Lord Lander," he said. "I shall have to ask you to come to Saville Row Police Station with me," and to the driver, "OK Sergeant, you can stop playing cabbie, the Commander wants to get some sleep tonight!"

Lander's mouth opened and then closed. He said nothing, he was dumbfounded. His arrest came as a complete surprise.

*

Commander Burt puffed on his pipe and looked over the expanse of Lake Geneva. His hotel boasted long French windows which gave him this wonderful view in the gathering dusk. He could see the lights from other lakeside hotels at varying distances dotted around the huge lake. They appeared like stars in the earth's atmosphere. He wondered when Jameson would get to the rendezvous, not knowing that two hours ago Jameson's borrowed VW had crossed the border into Switzerland. Mark Coggin had lain face down on the floor of the vehicle with Leanna Erhardt's long dresses and Jameson's shirts hanging from the travelling hooks covering him.

The Customs' Official's smile had been as diplomatic as Jameson's passport as he'd said:

"I see you're official sir, but may I ask about madam?"

"You may," replied Jameson icily. "She is my fiancée and we are passing through Switzerland to England where we are to be married at Cadbury Hall the day after tomorrow."

"Oh, I do beg your pardon sir, madam," said the official and returned the documents, hastily saluted and waved them on.

The crunching sound as Jameson engaged the gear coincided with Coggin's snort of constrained laughter as they moved off.

"Shut up Mark, for God's sake."

And to emphasise his point he stuffed a rolled sock into Coggin's open mouth.

It was nearly seven o'clock. Commander Burt had chosen the hotel half way round the Western side of the bowl of Lake Geneva because of its anonymity. It was well-staffed and run along American lines, as indeed most of its clientele were American businessmen staying with their wives, or meeting their Swiss business associates for business-cum-social reasons. Brookes Brothers suits and smart briefcases were common sights in the reception area.

Commander Burt rang for room service. He ordered a bottle of dry white wine, and when it came, ordered it to be placed up on the nearby table.

"Yes sir," a familiar voice said, "shall I pour you a glass?"

"Jameson, you fool," replied Burt. "Where have you been? I was beginning to think something had happened to you. And where's Coggin and the girl?" he asked anxiously.

"It's OK, they're downstairs. I just thought we might have ten minutes together first."

"Yes. Agreed. I've got some things to tell you!"

The Commander's face became vexed as he listened to Jameson's story.

"Now I am going to have to explain to our Austrian colleagues why you used their territory as a battleground," he said, "and you realise why Coggin insisted on Switzerland, don't you?"

"Of course," replied Peter Jameson. "He's committed no crime in Switzerland so we could find it difficult to extradite him from Swiss territory."

"Exactly. Now listen."

Swiftly he recounted to Jameson what had happened after his visit to Anna and the Fanlight Club.

"Lander, of course," Jameson said. "We were so busy chasing around after Coggin that we missed the obvious. Now it seems Coggin has fallen from favour in all directions. The Czechs want him, you want him, and the Austrians want him and the Americans would want him if they knew what we know. That's why he needs a deal."

"Yes and I shouldn't think it'll be long before the Americans join the queue. Do you know what he wants?" asked the Commander.

"No, not exactly, but I can guess. A ticket to Brazil or somewhere alike, money, a new identity, immunity from any charges – something along those lines. Will he get it?"

The Commander nodded.

"He'll get it if he delivers the goods. I dare not, not co-operate with the Americans on this one. No matter what Coggin's done. They are desperate for the identity of the man known as HH."

"Well you'd better see him sir. I must say he's very confident. I'll go and fetch him."

*

Leanna Erhardt sat in the hotel bar trying to make polite conversation with Jameson while they waited for the summons from Commander Burt. It seemed like an eternity. Half heartedly they talked, but discussion dwindled as they both knew that whatever they were talking about would cease as soon as that buzz on the bleeper in Peter Jameson's pocket came. It happened just as Jameson was beginning to become concerned for Commander Burt's safety. He had reasoned to himself as to what kind of an agent, even a reluctant one, leaves the top man of British Security alone and unprotected with a known double agent. To cover his concern he excused himself and went to the men's room, more as a result of restlessness than biological necessity. The double buzz came with such ferocity that Jameson almost forgot to re-zip his fly in his haste to rejoin Leanna and get to that suite on the fourth floor. A double bleep meant urgency. Without appearing hurried, he was at Leanna's side within fifteen seconds of the summons.

"Quickly," he said to her and threw several hundred franc notes on the table to cover the waiting extravagances, caught her hand, then sped in the direction of the lift.

Pulling Leanna behind him they reached the fourth floor, and he opened the door not knowing what to expect. They entered the suite. The two men, Commander Burt and Mark Coggin, stood facing Jameson with their backs to the French windows.

"Sunshine," said Coggin, "your shining knight's armour is showing. Come on in."

Jameson was beginning to find Coggin's feeble banter tiresome. He'd killed people to get this objectionable man to his boss. Before he could open his mouth Burt spoke.

"The lady behind you, Jameson, must be Miss Erhardt, whom I haven't had the pleasure of meeting in person although of course I've seen her name on reports, codename Ameli. And I must say," he said gallantly, "she more than does justice to those reports! You know, Jameson, a consistent factor in the jobs you've done for us is the fact that somehow attractive women appear on the scene."

Jameson said nothing. He felt there was no answer required by that statement.

"Down to business. Come and sit down," said the Commander. He turned to Coggin and said tersely, "I hope you realise that I am agreeing to your proposals reluctantly, and, it goes without saying, provided that you keep to your side of the agreement. And Jameson will ensure that you do."

They sat around the table. It looked like an unofficial directors meeting. But they were deciding upon much more important measures than what dividends should be paid to shareholders.

Commander Burt addressed the two field operatives.

"I've had quite a frank discussion with Mr Coggin and I believe we have a basis upon which we can do business. He knows that we have Lord Lander in jail, but it seems he has taken precautions to save his own skin. In return for what he wants," he looked at Coggin, and the corner of the left side of his mouth twitched upwards "a plastic surgeon's job on his face."

Coggin bent his head forward in half a bow.

"Five hundred thousand American dollars, and a one way ticket to South Africa. Oh, and one more thing."

A whimsical smile actually appeared on Burt's face.

"He wants a clean disappearance, no parking tickets etc. Although why he should worry about those, I don't understand."

"Maybe he's got a streak of decency in him," said Jameson slyly.

"Which is more than you have, judging by the way you knocked off those Czechs." Burt responded.

Jameson spread his hands, palms uppermost. "You wanted him," he nodded in Coggin's direction, "unharmed by the Eastern Europeans. It was the only way I could guarrantee you that."

"Mr Coggin," continued Commander Burt, "is concerned that we keep our part of the agreement, but because of his status with the CIA he won't deal with them directly. I have agreed that we will act as agents, a clearing house, and when I hear from you that you have in your safe possession the true identity of HH backed by documentary evidence, then I will see to it that Mr Coggin's terms are met."

"And where will this exchange take place, here?" asked Jameson.

"No, in St Moritz. Mr Coggin informs me that HH likes to spend Christmas there. There he will identify him. Oh, and by the way, Jameson, Mr Coggin is insisting that no other agents are involved. So you will be on your own with Miss Erhardt."

"There's one other thing," and now the Commander dropped an unexpected bombshell, "Mr Coggin wants her to accompany him as safekeeping to his point of departure."

He spoke as if Erhardt had not been there in the room with them.

"If you don't agree, Leanna," said Coggin, "I'll need to find some other form of insurance, but you'll be quite safe as long as nobody tries anything. After all," now he was speaking to Burt, "you've nothing to gain in my life for hers!"

Leanna Erhardt nodded immediately, "It's quite alright," she said. "I've had to do worse things, ask Jameson. Does my department know?"

The Commander shook his head.

"Nobody knows, except a few top people in Washington who will have to know to authorise the deal, and us. Even our Cabinet is in the dark."

Jameson could not resist, "And that's nothing unusual."

Burt turned to Leanna Erhardt.

"Miss Erhardt perhaps you would be kind enough to take Mr Coggin to the bar for a drink."

He turned to Mark Coggin. "Jameson and I have some details of your payoff, your identity change and your exit route to discuss which I'm sure you'll understand at this stage must be confidential. But don't concern yourself unduly. If I had some elaborate double cross plan in mind I certainly wouldn't make it as obvious as this."

"I'm sure you wouldn't Commander, and under the circumstances it's been a pleasure to do business with you. But I hope you won't change your mind. Jameson's a very good man, and you'd have a difficult job explaining the loss of Miss Erhardt to the Germans."

When the door had closed behind the others, Commander Burt went into details.

A coded call to London would assure them that Jameson had the information they required in a safe place. London would arrange for the money, half in cash and half drawn to cash on a Johannesburg bank, would be at the airport. Leanna would drive the car with Coggin to Zurich where Coggin's documents for his new identity would be awaiting. Coggin would fly on a scheduled flight to Johannesburg where a plastic surgeon would be available to perform the minor operation required to transform the face of Mark Coggin.

"And I hope that's the last we'll hear of him," said Burt. "I don't like him getting away with what he has done but there's a tremendous flap over in the States. It's really important to them to get to grips with HH. When I mention money they won't quibble - they'll give me *carte blanche*. Now you be careful, he's a tricky one is Coggin and I've a feeling he will try something. I'd look an awful idiot if he was setting us up to sell us a phoney."

"Don't worry, sir. I'll keep my wits about me."

The three left for St Moritz the next morning. Coggin insisted on buying a long furry pair of boots to replace the paper thin shoes he'd previously worn. It would take them at least three hours to get there as it had begun to snow heavily again. This time the snow was powder snow which would stick to the mountainous roads they had to take in order to reach the very fashionable resort of St Moritz.

Chapter 14
Winter Wonderland – St Moritz

They arrived in St Moritz mid-afternoon and drove to the resort's most well known hotel, The Palace.

At this time of year its internationally famous occupants would be on the ski slopes until five o'clock when they would troop in, still clad in their ski clothes, heavy ski boots and all, for the 'Apres ski five o'clock Tea Dance'.

Jameson noticed Gunter Sachs, boss of the giant ball bearing company and former husband of Bridgette Bardot, talking to Jimmy, leader of the Raquets pop group. The group would be performing for the hotel's famous clientele for the Tea Dance (between 5 and 7 p.m.) as they had done for the last three years. Jameson knew Jimmy well, and Sachs slightly, but it did not suit his purpose to have their presence in St Moritz discussed. The international set are a very cliquey crowd who know and follow one another throughout the year from one resort to another. He made his way unobtrusively to reception to lay claim to the two rooms the Commander had miraculously obtained for them, and then returned to the car where Leanna Erhardt and Coggin waited. Despatching the girl and Mark Coggin with the luggage, Peter Jameson made the pretence of taking the car to be garaged, but in fact drove swiftly out of town to a tiny village six kilometres west of St Moritz. He stopped his car outside a homely farmhouse and went inside. Here was another facet in the accommodation business. At The Palace the rooms were costing £650+ per day whereas here you could pay £40 per day. However, a tourist would be unlikely to find the place. You had to be in the know, or taken by someone who knew someone, and then also be prepared to share all accommodation other than your bedroom with the other occupants of the establishment. Each party provided its own food.

"Ah, the crazy Englishman," said the well-rounded, long-skirted woman in her mid sixties, who detached herself from the half dozen people seated around the communal table and came to greet him as Jameson opened the door. It was two years since Peter Jameson had last stayed with her, when he'd shared the accommodation for four days with a party of very loud German tourists. On the fourth day Jameson confided to his landlady what he had done to their breakfast. He had mixed toothpaste and another ill-tasting ingredient with their cream cheese rolls, and put a mixture of cod liver oil and soap in their jar of pickles. He and the landlady had sat back with innocent expressions on their faces to wait for contorted looks of disgust to appear on the Germans' faces. To their utter amazement every morsel was eaten with relish. One of the wives was even heard to say 'delicious' as she licked her fingers. Jameson smiled as he shook the old landlady's hand.

"You remember me then," he said.

"Of course, *Mein Fruhstuck* chef," and she laughed heartily, the effort shaking her matronly bosom. "But this time my friend, no tricks! They're all nice people." And she wagged a mock warning finger at him.

"No, no Frau Sattler," he said, remembering the serious task ahead of him, "this time I'm working. I've some investigative journalism to do for an English newspaper, and shouldn't think I'll have time for pranks. I'd be obliged if you'd keep my stay here a secret from any strangers enquiring about me. No, of course, I've done nothing wrong... Yes, I have a girl with me... No, not the same one as last time... Yes, another German girl... Yes, the other one was very nice but something just went wrong... Let's just say we became too used to one another." He rattled off answers to Frau Sattler's barrage of questions. He left the farmhouse as quickly as he had arrived. He would have no problems with his hideaway. Frau Sattler retired early and the house was left unlocked for guests to come and go as they pleased, as is the way with mountain people.

Mark Coggin paid only casual attention to Leanna Erhardt's spasmodic questions, as he considered his situation. As far as he knew he was the only person who had seen HH and could say "That man is HH." Even Lord Lander, who had been Coggin's US contact and now languished in jail, had not penetrated this secret. Inspector Fisher's death had been of significance. Coggin had found out because HH's bodyguard had killed Inspector Fisher in his lonely cubby-hole in the Yorkshire hotel in England.

*

After HH had despatched his entourage to return with his private jet from Yeadon Airport, HH and Coggin had made their way to Bradford Station. HH remained unobtrusively in the background while Coggin purchased tickets to London, rightly reasoning that boat-train tickets to Dover late in November from Bradford stood a good chance of being remembered, whereas from the main Continental Ticket Office in Sloane Street, London, there would be little or no chance of this happening. They boarded the London-bound express and found themselves an empty compartment. Shortly after the train had begun to gather speed HH swung his handcase from the luggage rack and disappeared in the direction of the washroom to freshen up.

Coggin dozed, but after half an hour or so was awoken by the opening of the sliding door and the entrance of a youngish man of around thirty-five to forty, not the ticket inspector Coggin expected. He had a shock of mousy-coloured hair with an unruly tuft at the front, a smooth complexion, and when he spoke he revealed large front teeth and a deep New England, American accent.

"It's cold and wet over here in England isn't it?" he said conversationally. "My name's Ben Johnson by the way," and extended his hand.

Coggin replied to the effect that it was always cold and wet in England in the winter, and they conversed politely until Doncaster. The young man, who had told Mark Coggin that he was touring England, Scotland and Wales by train before going to St Moritz where he always spent the New Year, got to his feet as the train slowed for the station and put on the casual sports jacket he'd laid on the seat.

"Sir," he said, "this is where I get off', and once again extending his hand to Coggin said, "it's been a real pleasure talking to you. You have a good trip now," and left.

The train gathered speed again and the ticket inspector appeared at the door. However, he did not ask for tickets but handed Mark Coggin an envelope.

"A gentleman asked me to bring you this, sir," he said.

Puzzled and somewhat fearful under the circumstances, Coggin took the envelope and muttered, "Thanks."

He waited until the official had left before slitting the envelope with his forefinger. It contained a hand-written note bearing the signature, 'HH'. The note read: 'Mark, I thought it could be kinda dangerous for us both to travel together in view of the present circumstances, so I am taking another train from Leeds to travel independently. You proceed with your normal travel arrangements and I will meet you at Brown's Hotel in Vienna in two days. Destroy this and good luck. HH.'

But Mark Coggin had not destroyed the letter and it was to form part of the evidence which would reveal the true identity of HH. But as he sat waiting for Jameson to return from the parking of the car in St Moritz, this was not Coggin's main cause for concern. How could he be absolutely sure the British and/or Americans would not double cross him after he had revealed the information they so desperately wanted. He pondered the problem for some time and then the glimmer of an idea came to his cunning brain. He was playing the desperate game of a gambler who thought he held all the right cards, but could not be one hundred per cent confident until the final card was laid on the table. When he saw that final card, either tomorrow or the next day, he would produce his ace and put his plan into operation. He would assure himself of the visual identity in the area where ski-jumpers queue for the chair lifts to take them to the Olympic ski-jump slope where the amateurs Christmas ski jump contest was to take place. Unless Mark Coggin was miles out in his thinking, HH would be there contesting. It was then that he would need to arrange for his insurance. If he was wrong he knew he could very quickly become a dead man.

The British could try him for treason, or kill him. The Americans would also be more than happy to have him removed from the face of God's earth, and the Russians had already demonstrated their desire for his presence in their territory, dead or alive. In fact, Coggin thought idly, he'd fancy his chances as slightly better with the East than with the West and he idly considered offering his services to Gadaffi. But he pulled himself together with a jolt as Jameson came into the room. He wasn't wrong – he couldn't be!

"Sorry I was so long Leanna," Jameson lied. "I needed some cigarettes and bumped into the Pradda from Kitzbuhel at the cigarette kiosk and he kept me talking all this time."

The man he mentioned specialised in making ski outfits for the very famous and his workshop would make to his design and personally measured and supervised by him an outfit in twenty-four hours. The explanation appeared to satisfy Coggin, and Jameson continued.

"Now then, Mark. How do you propose for us to play this little game?"

"OK, sunshine, don't rush me. One step at a time. I have to be very careful or (a) you won't get your man, and (b) what's important to me, I won't get the deal I agreed with your Commander."

"Whatever the Commander has said he'll honour," said Jameson with a conviction which he had to admit he did not really feel inside. Coggin eyed them both speculatively and continued.

"It's very important to keep a low profile at this place because our man will certainly stay here when he arrives." He yawned. "I don't know about you two, but I shall be having a drink sent to my room, and then early to bed. We have to be early on the ski slopes in the morning. Shall we say breakfast in your room, it's larger, at 7a.m.?"

They nodded and he left them.

Swiftly Jameson explained to Leanna the preparations he'd made.

"So if anything happens to me make for there, OK? Frau Sattler is a good friend of mine. She'll look after you."

Chapter 15

Double-Cross

At the tiny ski-hire chalet Mark Coggin, who was not a skier, explained that he would require only the heavy ski boots with steel heels and toes. In good weather conditions, they were cumbersome but they were almost a necessity in the heavy snow conditions currently being experienced in St Moritz. Silently, save for the scrunch of their boots in the snow, the trio filed through the narrow streets together with the throng of early morning skiers, who with their skis perched on their shoulders were progressing happily towards the main *kabel bahn*. There, huge gondolas transported approximately sixty people at a time, high up the mountain to their first leg of the ascent. At this level average skiers enjoyed their sport, while the more proficient, or ambitious, went higher via T Bars. It was at this first station that Mark Coggin planned on keeping watch. In order to reach the Olympic ski jump run, all the contestants had to pass through this station. They sat, the three of them, in the corner of the restaurant drinking coffee. After a while Jameson became tired of asking Coggin if the man they were seeking was one of the new arrivals constantly passing through this key station.

"For God's sake, why don't you two go and ski?" said Coggin. "I can't do anything with you here and I'm not about to touch him on the shoulder if he does come! Where's the percentage in that for me? And, he may not come until tomorrow."

His logic seemed to make some sense, especially as Jameson had not formulated an immediate plan of action should Coggin even say to him, "That's the man." There would be time enough for him to think and plan as the situation developed. However, he thought it was not going to be as easy as that to prise the man's identity out of Mark Coggin even after he had him positively identified. No, he felt it would do no harm for them to relax on the ski slopes.

"OK, Mark," he said, "good idea."

"Good thinking, Mr Jameson," said Leanna Erhardt light-heartedly, eyebrows raised questioningly after they were perched on the T Bar together, being propelled steadily aloft. Their skis travelled automatically in the tracks of others, like trains crossing the points. "You decided to give Mr Coggin, I think the English expression is, a little rope?"

"Yes, but in this case I hope, enough of it to hang HH too! I'm more than curious to discover what those initials stand for, and who he is. I got a feeling Mark Coggin doesn't know for certain either, that's why he wants us out of the way!"

"You mean while he makes a positive ID?"

"That's right."

*

The cable cars were arriving steadily now, every eight or ten minutes, as Coggin swiftly examined the occupants of each one before they moved along to the higher bound car for the ski jump.

Another car arrived, and its door jerked open. The first man out was his man. Coggin watched him, a feeling of satisfaction coming over him. The feeling a result of the fact that he had speculated on a hunch backed by coincidence, some facts, and his gambler's judgement. Now the feeling of satisfaction turned to alarm, because the four men in his quarry's party were coming into the restaurant. Their heads were turned towards one another and they were in boisterous conversation, they had not seen him, but they were walking straight towards him. Desperately he picked up the newspaper which was lying on the next table and held it in front of him.

"I agree with Ted," that name was further confirmation should Coggin have needed it, the strong nasal tones of one of the quartet said. "You jump much better after an early morning Schnapps."

Fortunately for Coggin the Americans chose the opposite corner and Coggin stole a glance over his newspaper at them. They were a fit-looking bunch. All built like college footballers. The one Coggin was examining as closely as he dared had the boyish face, large teeth and unruly hair of the man who'd introduced himself to Mark Coggin on the Yorkshire Express as Ben Johnson. No wonder HH was such a mysterious figure, he was never seen unless he was carefully disguised. And Coggin had to admit that the man he was furtively studying bore no resemblance at all to the man HH, in whose company Coggin had been many times.

He cast his mind back to that Yorkshire to London Express. The man who'd then called himself Ben Johnson had undoubtedly been testing him. Had Coggin shown a hint of recognition he would have been killed and thrown from the train, of this he had no doubt. And yet, ironically, without realising it at that time, the first inconsistency surrounding the mystery of HH had entered Mark Coggin's head. He'd wondered why the young American with an accent denoting that he came from the wealthy New England area, had no coat with him in the wilds of Yorkshire, in the middle of winter.

Coggin would probably never have thought to compare ears, had not HH a habit that Coggin had noticed for the first time when they'd met at their predetermined venue in Vienna, a habit of pulling and rubbing the right lobe of his ear with thumb and forefinger, and completing the action by running the thumb and forefinger in a 'V' from the cheek bones to stroke either side of the jaw line to his chin. He'd seen someone else do that very recently, but he had not remembered who, until the day after HH had left Vienna for America. As soon as the picture of Ben Johnson sitting opposite him pulling and rubbing his ear and chin had leapt before his eyes, the incidence of the coat and the departure of HH and Ben Johnson at Doncaster (a coal mining town rather than a tourist spot), it did not take Coggin long to guess the truth.

Then it was that the difficult task was presented to him. How to go about finding who Ben Johnson was, and proving it. Once he'd done all that he had to find a foolproof way of getting his information together factually on paper, and setting up the deal which would get him off the hook and provide money for early retirement. No mean task but he was now within an ace of accomplishing the grand slam.

He waited tensely as the four Americans sat at the table no more than ten yards away, these were anxious moments for him. His heart missed a beat every time the restaurant door opened. It would be cruel luck if Jameson and the Erhardt woman came barging in or that Ben Johnson or HH, whoever he was, should come over for a light, an ashtray, sugar or something equally ridiculous. But nothing like that happened. In the fullness of time the four Americans paid their bill and laughingly left the restaurant. After sufficient time had elapsed for them to get clear, Coggin called the waitress, paid his bill and hurried outside to catch the next descending cable car.

He could hardly wait for the cable car to bump against the lower landing and he hurried to the Palace Hotel. Pushing the revolving door impatiently, Coggin made his way to reception. One of the rules of etiquette strictly enforced by the management was that every guest sign the visitor's book personally, with details of their last stop-over. The assistant manager approached Coggin.

"Can I be of any assistance to you, sir?" he asked.

"Yes. I'd like to check if a friend of mine has arrived. May I see the visitor's book?"

"Certainly, sir," the man replied and he pushed the book in Coggin's direction, and moved away to assist an elderly Swiss lady.

Coggin spread the note written by HH on the Yorkshire Pullman inside the register and ran his finger down the column of recent arrivals. Finally he found the handwriting he sought. But the name that stared starkly back at him bordered on the bounds of impossibility, and as recognition dawned on him, he could hardly believe it. He checked the handwriting as carefully as possible against every other entry, but there was no mistake. Thoughtfully he copied the name and address from the register and closed the book. He was still gazing into space trying to comprehend the enormity of his discovery when the voice of the assistant manager interrupted his chain of thought, thus bringing him back to reality.

"Find what you wanted, sir?" he asked.

"Yes thank you. Yes, I certainly did. Now, one more thing. Where's the gents lavatory?"

"The gentlemen's cloakroom," replied the man haughtily, as only assistant managers can, "is over there in the right hand corner by the entrance," he indicated the direction with his eyes.

"Thanks," said Coggin, the man moved away.

Coggin helped himself to several sheets of the hotel's note paper, an envelope, and also a magazine, then he headed in the indicated direction. It was a relatively quiet time of the day as Coggin found a cubicle and began to write. It was time to commit all he knew to paper. The task took him almost an hour, as he explained his entire knowledge of HH. He recorded HH's circumstantial boastings on the multi-million treasury manipulations, and added to this his own knowledge of those officials who had collaborated in that department. He dealt with the evidence he had that HH had worked with the Russians.

He gave the address at which could be found his secret document case which contained evidence substantiating all this.

This evidence damned the mysterious HH, but as the man had never been seen by anyone else without disguise, he could once again slip away into obscurity. But now Mark Coggin knew who he really was. What Coggin had written up to this stage would be of tremendous value to both the British and the American Governments. On its own it was worth the price Coggin was demanding for his freedom. But it was penny ante stuff compared with the final page of Coggin's document.

When the name he now wrote down with the details of how he'd made his discovery became known throughout the world, chaos would reign. Coggin wondered as he described how he'd discovered that the mysterious American would be at St Moritz thus enabling Coggin to finally denounce him, how would the two nations, Britain and America, handle it? They couldn't just let the information hit the streets as newspaper and television headlines! Whole banks would collapse overnight, shares in companies could become worthless, certain nations could become bankrupt and it might even provoke a war. It was not as if it could just be dismissed as one man's unsubstantiated story, in the document Coggin now finalised were the hard facts.

Now Coggin knew the name behind the face, and he had the full documentary evidence, including fingerprints and handwriting. He decided there and then to ask for a million. How the authorities handled his information was their problem. He'd be safely tucked away with a new identity. He signed the document with a flourish, enclosed the HH letter and addressed the envelope. He stretched and unlocked the closet door. As an afterthought he walked back and flushed the toilet and left a ten franc note on the empty attendant's plate. After all, it was a cheap price to pay for the office where he had put the finishing touches to a presentation which would net him a profit of a cool one million pounds.

After that he returned to the reception hall where he purchased a stamp for the letter and dropped it in the post box. With this accomplished, he felt relieved as the document he'd just mailed was, he considered, dynamite, and he was glad to get it out of his possession. Mark Coggin was sitting comfortably in the bar enjoying his first drink as Jameson and Leanna Erhardt discovered his absence from the corner seat of the mountain restaurant.

With the initial shock and a slight feeling of panic over, Jameson sat down to think.

"No Coggin! Where has he gone? Only one way to find out, ski down the mountain and look for him."

"Fancy a *Gluh Wein*?" Leanna Erhardt asked him.

"Just right," he replied. "It'll warm us up and we'll ski that much faster to the bottom."

She disappeared to search out the waitress who was snatching a belated lunch behind a screen. When she returned Jameson said, "You know Leanna, I think this is not the disaster situation we first thought."

She raised her eyebrows inquiringly.

"Well, look at it this way. Until today we've been sticking to Coggin like glue. Not giving him an inch in which to move and generally looking over his shoulder the whole time. So he sent us off to ski expecting something to happen! It must have happened. I think he is just beginning to play his hand, which means we might start to find things out."

The *Gluh Wein* arrived steaming hot, with its fruity flavour and overriding taste of cloves. They sipped the tasty drink and he continued.

"Let's start to make him think a bit. When we get to the foot of the ski run, you take the car and go to see Frau Sattler at the farmhouse. Familiarise yourself with her and the area; it might be useful before we're finished here. I'll find Mark and try to sound him out to see if he has identified HH yet, and if he's got the evidence we need and he promised. I'll ply him with a few drinks, you know, generally play it by ear.

"He may well open up with just me on my own, even if he just pointed to somebody and said, that's him. I've still got to have the evidence, and from the way it seems the Americans are behaving, the thing's big, very big, which means substantial evidence."

"America is so far away and is so vast, it's difficult to know what they think. You know, when I was a little girl I was brought up to believe they were all crooks and gangsters over there."

"That might not have been so far wrong from where we are standing," he said, but he had a smile on his face. "Come on, let's get down this mountain, I see the clouds coming down!"

They skied swiftly and uneventfully to the foot of the mountain and as they prepared to go their separate ways she asked, "By the way Peter, you never did tell me why you became a disc jockey?"

"Oh, didn't I?" He said over his shoulder. "For the same reason every disc jockey does. I like the sound of my own voice. All right!?

"Now, why did you start life modelling bikinis Leanna?"

"If I told you it was because I fancied my own body, it would sound equally strange would it not?" She said, and making a swift parallel turn on her skis by way of a classic stop she ended up facing Jameson, and sending a contrived slipstream of snow into his face.

Jameson turned and snowplowed gently down the slight gradient which led from the ski slopes into town to commence his search for Mark Coggin. He had a feeling that that gentleman would not be far from the Palace Hotel. That was if his assessment of the situation was on the right lines.

*

"You'll frequently find Coggin in bed, if he wants to keep out of the way," came the words from the direction of Mark Coggin's bed, as Jameson stealthily entered his bedroom. Peter Jameson walked over to the curtains and ripped them open, allowing in the last vestiges of daylight.

"Come on, Mark," he said. "This is no time to get pissed for anyone's sake. Tell me, what's happening? Did you see him? Where's your professionalism?"

Although Jameson feigned exasperation he secretly thought that Coggin had made the necessary identification.

"Oh, no, sunshine," Coggin had enjoyed an extended lunchtime bar session to the limit. "I've got it all worked out for you and me! That's why I'm pissed! You'll be the bloody hero, and I'll get the money."

"A hero! Well, perhaps you'd be good enough to let me know the extent of my heroics, so that I can decide. I've got orders you know, and they are to find out the identity of HH. You agreed to this. The sooner you hand me the evidence or tell me where it is, complete with his identity, then the sooner London will be contacted by me and your escape plan, your cash bonanza and arrangements for a new ID, will be set in motion."

"All in good time. All in good time, sunshine. I've got all the evidence you need in a safe place and believe me this thing's bigger than anybody thinks." He chuckled wisely.

"Well, when is this great revelation going to take place? If you've got it, let's have it!"

"Oh, not so fast sunshine. I've got my insurance to think of. You'll know soon enough, probably tomorrow. Now then, get out of here an' let me have a lil' sleep, unless you've brought a drink with you. An' close those damned curtains."

He turned over to avoid the intrusion of light, and Jameson left the room. As he walked thoughtfully to the lift, Jameson had the uneasy feeling that things were not going as well for him as they should. He was being manoeuvred and he didn't like to be manoeuvred, but he didn't see what he could do short of trying to force the information out of Coggin. And Coggin, either by accident or design, would not be of much use to anyone before he sobered up. At a rough estimate, Jameson thought this would not be much before dinner time which would be as good a time as any considering the hangover Coggin should have. The thought brought a wintry smile which would have matched the St Moritz scene outside, to Jameson's features.

Chapter 16
Vital Information

At the turn of the year, London can be a mixture of all the seasons, but this one was cold, chilly and decidedly autumnal. And it was Anna Dubric who was the Songstress Nightingale, she sang so sweetly for Special Branch from Berkeley Square all that season that the well-known song could have been written for her! Although the Sweeney/O'Hara bombing campaign was operated with Capone-style efficiency, her informative output from Berkeley Square offices had enabled bombs to be distinguished from hoaxes and the real ones accurately located. Dubric had begun to feel an accomplished spy until Sweeney asked her point blank one day, if she had any idea how Scotland Yard could be locating their devices so quickly. It had been Bob Sweeney who Anna Dubric had chosen to pay special attention to at the Fanlight Club, having insider knowledge of his fancies she had found him easier, both by comparison, and on the eye, than Fat O'Hara to milk for information. Dubric hoped she had deflected attention from herself, and furthered her own cause by offering callous advice in answer to this question, and afterwards turned over in her mind jubilantly the significance of what had followed.

"I don't know why you give them any warnings at all Bob," she'd said brashly. "I wouldn't! If you're in a killing situation... you kill! The communists taught us that when I was a girl in Czechoslovakia. But if politics says warnings be given, and they're being found too quickly – halve the time. Get the pigs snorting a bit for starters, eh!"

At that joke Sweeney had laughed and replied, "Communism and terrorism are pretty similar Anna. The two isms go hand in hand." He'd squeezed her hand, "I guess that's why that makes you one of us," he grinned, "that and the way you're stacked baby!" He'd then continued confidingly. "The situation never arises with our Hammas connection in the Middle East. They don't ponce about, they just hit the wrong spots, and at the moment in the wrong country! So the Middle East marriage Coggin brokered will be a brilliant exercise now we're doin' it, because what we've..."

"Got some f*****g work to do! You wanna' come into the office now Bob?" The irritated voice interrupting, speaking on the reception desk intercom, was O'Hara's who said witheringly, "We got a shippin' schedule to work out, with a big laundry attachment on it for Libya, right! A million bucks! You can shoot the breeze with Anna later 'cos that's all you two seem to shoot, breeze! You'll keep won't you honey?... But our friend comin' in for his dhobi won't. He'll expect everything ready for him, and neatly packaged, and that includes some nooky from the Fanlight. Your department Anna. C'mn Sweeney. Get your arse in here!"

"Right Joe." Dutifully Sweeney got up and left.

After Sweeney had disappeared through the red door Anna Dubric breathed a temporary sight of relief, because she always felt more endangered with O'Hara than with Sweeney, and then pressed the red record button under her desk. She knew enough about Middle East jargon to know that dhobi was an old army slang term for laundry, and then well... everyone knew about money laundering. And somebody important from the Middle East was coming in to collect some! Sweeney, in his efforts to show her how big time he was, had practically confessed to a major new development in that area originated by the missing Mark Coggin! So what she knew and what she expected to find out would urgently need to be transmitted to Peter Jameson. She would know soon enough who the Middle

East man was because their penises are never far from their brains, and it would fall to her to arrange his female company.

So it was loud alarm bells that rang two days later for Anna Dubric when she entered Berkeley Square House at 10 a.m. An Arab man who had been studying the building index approached her, and when Dubric saw who he was her heart skipped several beats. She had met this man several times, sometimes alone, but usually in the company of Mark Coggin at the Fanlight Club. There was no sign of recognition now on the man's face as he politely asked, if she knew where the firm O'Hara Arms Sales was! Smiling at the thoughts of O'Hara dispensing limbs to malformed Arabs, Dubric introduced herself as Miss Dubrey and escorted the man to the office suite which occupied the entire fifth floor. 'So this was the Middle East connection arriving,' thought Anna. A face she knew well, but of her he had no recollection. 'Thank God for the truth of the claims that hostesses are only for companionship if they don't remember their faces,' she thought. Bidding him to accompany her when she'd introduced herself as Miss Dubrey, they ascended fifth-floorwards in the elevator. During this time, which seemed an eternity to 'Anne Dubrey', she wisely kept her own council, trusting to her street clothes for disguise and that a chance word would not jog a memory. O'Hara had no booked appointment, and she had never known O'Hara or Sweeney to get into the office at 10 a.m.! However, O'Hara was there and greeted his visitor warmly with a, "Good to see you again Shaheen," (Dubric knew the man as Abdul) and a, "you come right in now."

Very much later that night a suitably attired Anna Dubric returned to Berkeley Square House. She ascended by lift to the fifth floor, where she let herself into the now deserted offices of Benson's, and seated herself at her reception desk. Cautiously she withdrew the secret contents of her bottom drawer and began to listen. Two hours later she left with the Winston Churchill paperweight neatly packaged and headed for the all night post office in Trafalgar Square.

"Who says there ain't no Santa Claus?" she said to the friendly night man, who responded with a ready smile.

"I would very much like to be going where it's going, ma'am," he said.

Chapter 17

Callahan

Senator Edward Callahan loved St Moritz. It suited a lifestyle he favoured in America, but found difficult to accomplish there except in a simulated form. The people around him here were real people, not movie producers or business manipulators. They came from generations of wealth and fulfilment. Not for them the soiling of their hands with work. This was done for them by the people they employed, who were only too happy to play at companies and leave their masters free to get on with the much more serious business of living. Callahan was the youngest son of Jo Callahan, an Irish immigrant who had arrived in Chicago in the early thirties. Unlike most immigrants he did not arrive without some money. During this depressed period he was able to use his money to buy buildings, on occasions for as little as 5% of their true value. Jo Callahan made many enemies on his way to success. The way he treated people, mercilessly foreclosing on all debtors who could not meet their commitments, did not endear him to many poor people's hearts. He tackled small people at first as they had the softest voices, and sometimes forced whole families out on to the streets. In those days there was scant protection from the law. Callahan thrived during this depressed period. He would say he invested wisely and built an empire by hard work and careful planning. Others would say he ruthlessly exploited people and their unfortunate circumstances. His residential empire grew, and when he was worth ten million dollars he decided to move into the exploitation of the business sector by using gangsters' extortion methods prevalent in the pre-war era.

By this time he had four sons and they had moved to Washington and although Callahan had political aspirations he knew that even with the immense wealth he was now amassing he had not been born in the country and could only exert his influence from behind the scenes, which he did. Huge government contracts were awarded to his companies without more than a handful of people even being aware that they had been awarded to a Callahan company brought for next to nothing. But Jo Callahan's political dream was insatiable. His sons would go into politics. The coming of war brought him more wealth and his first personal grief. His eldest son was killed in the Battle of Britain flying for the Royal Air Force, this had the effect of souring Callahan's attitude to the British. He blamed this loss on Great Britain and never forgave them for taking from him the son whom he'd planned to install in the White House some day.

His second son, after a brilliant start to his early political career, had been the subject of a MacCarthy witch hunt smear campaign so familiar in the fifties. And Jo Callahan's enemies, who now numbered many, were quick to seize this opportunity to thwart him. His second son's life ended mysteriously with the Coroner recording an open verdict. Jo Callahan never really got over his son's death, it was openly rumoured that he drove his son to suicide, and shortly afterwards he suffered a stroke from which he never fully recovered, although he lived on a further ten years.

After his death, the remaining sons, Ronald and Edward, managed to shake off the Callahan stigma. With their now vast empire, they were able to hire the best PR firms in the country to improve the Callahan image. They were by now both actively involved in the only game they knew – power politics – and Ronald, after a volatile period in the house of Senate was poised for his attempt at the Presidency in next year's election.

Backed by the Callahan machine and big business, old Jo Callahan's dream was in sight.

Had he lived, he would have been proud of his son's achievements. And now the youngest Callahan, Edward, was doing what he had done each Christmas for the past five years, he was relaxing with his friends in St Moritz. There was never a shortage of feminine company for him or his friends and he was just preparing to join a small, arranged party in the hotel's Cliff Bar when there was a knock on his door.

"It's open," he called. "Just walk right in."

The blood drained from his face and the welcoming smile that he reserved for visiting friends dropped from his lips as Mark Coggin strode in.

"Evening Senator," said Coggin smugly.

Edward Callahan recovered himself quickly. It was inconceivable that this was happening to him but there was Coggin standing in front of him unannounced and a look of triumphant malevolence on his face. It was no use trying to bluster, the man knew his secret.

"How did you find out?" was all he could muster.

"Oh, a collection of little things, like your not having a coat, for instance, when you appeared in my carriage, travelling through Yorkshire and introducing yourself as Ben Johnson. Nobody travels in England in the middle of winter without a topcoat. You were trying to be a little too clever. You know, it's stretching coincidence that bit too far, for one American on an English train to disappear, only to be replaced by another American, however different. But I might not have become suspicious if you hadn't sent those Czech apes to get me. Nobody except you knew I was there. That's why I didn't obey their instructions in the note. As I just said, you blew it by just trying to be too clever, HH."

"What do you want? This has got to be a blackmail touch."

"That's rich coming from you. You've spent your life getting what you want by blackmail, in one form or another, and your father before you, and now you're condemning me when I come in for a small share. You're damn right, it is blackmail. I want a million pounds!"

Edward Callahan, alias Ben Johnson, alias HH, did not bat an eyelid at the terms. He'd learned the lesson of a cool reaction to an outrage.

"You've got it. How about guarantees?"

But Coggin sensed the man's temporary lack of confidence.

"Guarantees?"

"Yes, you don't think I'm going to let you walk away with a cool million without stringent guarantees of your silence, do you?"

Already the old Joe Callahan in his youngest son was starting to tick. There was only one way to buy silence and that was not with money. No, it certainly was not with money. Coggin would sell to the highest bidder, and would always be a threat as long as he lived. As long as he lived! As if to answer his unsaid question Coggin spoke.

"If you're thinking, Senator, that you could take care of things less expensively, forget it. If I don't appear tomorrow there's a British agent staying with me named Peter Jameson who will be in possession of as much information as I have," lied Coggin.

Callahan's brain worked quickly under such circumstances as these. Coggin was much too dangerous to be allowed to stay alive, but for the time being, for the sake of expediency, he'd have to play along with him. He'd no alternative. Even though his older brother knew nothing of his extra curricular activities, an Indian Chieftain would stand more chance of being elected the next President of the US than Ronald, if even a hint of this business leaked out. And, besides, the plan was that when his brother had finished his term as President, he would take over. No, Coggin had to be eliminated, and so it seemed would this Peter Jameson, but he had to be sure that he had halted the landslide of retribution which would undoubtedly be his if Coggin leaked his deadly information. He smiled easily at Coggin.

"I'm sure we can work together," he said. "I already had plans to move you up in the organisation. You know that. OK. So you need a million pounds to make you feel secure. I told you, you've got it. I can afford it."

"I was hoping you would feel this way, Senator," said Coggin taking the bait and swallowing it whole. "You know, there's one thing that's really been puzzling me."

"Oh, what's that?"

"Well, I could understand your being able to change your appearance, although that alone was a masterpiece, no one would ever have known, but how the hell did you do the voices? They're totally different."

Edward Callahan chuckled.

"That was the easiest part of all. It's a closely guarded actor's secret, but the way the majority of those very deep bass voices are produced from what is often a skinny little runt, is by using what is called a gurgle box."

"A gurgle box?"

"Yes, it's a tiny little battery operated microphone and amplifier combined, that sits neatly behind the front teeth," he pointed with his finger to his own teeth, "and when the voice goes through from the throat, it automatically deepens it, or it can be adjusted to produce any sound within the range."

"Incredible," Mark Coggin stared at him in near disbelief.

"Yes, it was invented by the same man who made the synthesiser, I finance him so I get to know his other tricks. When you think about it, the two inventions have similar overtones, if you'll excuse the pun!"

The two men looked at one another, Coggin trying to assess his chances with this man and Callahan attempting to exude trust, even though he knew without doubt that Coggin would be killed as soon as he could ensure that Coggin could no longer betray him.

Coggin broke the silence and thus, some would have it said, lost the psychological battle.

"If I'm hitching my wagon to yours, Senator," he said, "you're going to have to get me into the US and get me a new identity as I'm *persona non grata* here."

"No problem. I'm here with my own plane. The four guys with me went to Yale with me and they are now my official security guards," he chuckled. "Government jobs for the boys you see, we look after each other. So no immigration official will even bother to come near the plane. There will be a bunch of photographers when we land in New York, because it's election year. Part of the press build up, Americans love to relate, didn't you know."

Coggin nodded as Senator Edward Callahan went on.

"In the thirties and forties, the early movie days, it was film stars. All the guys walked around like John Wayne." He walked around the room giving a fair imitation of the famous cowboy's stiff-legged roll with arms dangling loosely by his thighs. "So now they're interested in politics. Us, the key men in each party, we're all coached in camera techniques, and I'll bet if I come anywhere at all in the ski jumping over here, they'll have shots on the TV news. No, don't worry about what happens when we get to the US, Mark. The US is my oyster."

"Well then, we are left now with one more very important detail. Jameson and the girl, Leanna Erhardt."

"Ah, yes of course, I was coming to that."

Callahan could not believe his good fortune. Coggin was playing headlong into his hands in offering up unasked the two people who tipped the balance in his favour.

"We'll have to deal with them personally," he said. "These people here with me know nothing about my private side. They're strictly friends and security."

Before he could say more, there was a knock on the door and in walked one of the most beautiful women Coggin had seen for a long time. Dark-haired, medium height and impeccably groomed; she was the sort of woman who went with this class of hotel. Her dark blue chiffon dress fitted snugly at the waist and accentuated the ample cleavage that required no supporting garment. Coggin took this all in at a glance as she came forward and in a delightfully foreign accent, probably Italian, thought Coggin, said, "Teddy, we wondered what had 'appened to you. The others all wait in the bar for you."

"Yes, I was just on my way right now. Oh, Mark, allow me to introduce Sofia."

The girl smiled politely as Coggin took her hand and briefly touched it with his lips. The solitaire diamond on the third finger of her hand almost leapt into his eye.

They moved towards the door and Callahan said casually,

"OK, Mark, we'll finalise that other matter tomorrow, shall we? How about having breakfast with me here?"

Coggin nodded, the die was cast, he'd just set up the biggest double cross of his entire lifetime.

"What time?" he asked.

"Shall we say 8.30?" Was the reply.

*

Leanna Erhardt sat at the friendly living room table at the Bauenhaus Sattler. She was in happy conversation with Frau Sattler who had taken to her immediately. As soon as Jameson walked in she could see there was something wrong by the expression on his face. He was not the sort of person to let things show. In fact she had once jokingly told him, 'You'd laugh at the devil while he slit your throat.'

On the pretext of having a walk in the frozen countryside to clear their heads, they slipped away.

"OK," she said as soon as they were outside, "what's wrong?"

"I'm not sure," he replied. "But Coggin's stalling. He's made a positive identification of HH, of that I'm pretty sure. He's as good as told me so, and he says he's going to hand the whole thing over to me on a plate, evidence and all, tomorrow or the next day. But I don't buy that. I think he is going to try to do a better deal with HH. In which case our lives will not be worth the proverbial rub."

She looked at him. "I could get help from our people. Within a few hours we could..."

"No," he interrupted. "Commander Burt specifically said, 'No other involvement'."

"Commander Burt's not here. And if you're right, we're likely to be wiped out by people we don't even know. The only one we know is Coggin, and he's keeping a very low profile."

Jameson was thoughtful for a few moments, the only sound was from their boots crunching into the frozen snow as they followed the country lane's winding pattern.

Then he said, "I've got an idea. Let's even the odds up a little. We'll stay out here tonight and maybe even tomorrow night if necessary, which will keep us out of Coggin's way. This'll surprise him as he's expecting me to be breathing down his neck and I won't even be around. But before we do that, you and I will go the Palace and we'll make a few modifications in our room."

Now that he'd thought of something positive to do he felt an excitement mounting inside him. He formulated his idea into a careful plan as Leanna drove the few kilometres to St Moritz. He checked the contents of the 'Q' kit and then explained to her his plan to even out the odds.

*

"Can't you stay with me all night, Teddy darling? Just this once?" Asked the lovely Sofia. Turning over in her bed, and rising on her elbow, she revealed a breathtaking half nude body as she reached out for the half empty champagne glass on her bedside table.

Edward Callahan looked longingly at her, how he would love to accept her offer. She was so desirable as she looked invitingly at him over the rim of her glass, her lips drawing a tiny trickle of the dry bubbling wine into her parched throat. But he had pressing work ahead of him that night and every moment he now delayed could be crucial.

"'Fraid not baby," he replied, "not tonight. I gotta grab some sack time. I've got this meeting in-" he glanced at his watch, "-oh, my God! See you tomorrow," and he straightened his tie, pressed his lips to hers and left her suite.

In response to the discreet enquiry with the desk clerk earlier that evening he'd been told that Mr Jameson was out at a private party and was not expected to return until at least three that morning.

Callahan now approached Jameson's bedroom door. A swift glance left and then right ensured that he would not be disturbed as he inserted a small blunt instrument into the lock. His heart raced, what if he was discovered? He had no weapon with him, as his St Moritz trip was not connected with his HH identity. The lock clicked and he stepped into the room and stood for a moment accustoming his eyes to the light. It was not pitch black as a very soft light filtered through the net curtain drapes illuminating objects in the room in eerie silhouettes. He stiffened, he could hear breathing. His eyes stared into the darkness towards the bed. He could see a shape. Jameson must have returned early. His eyes darted towards the dressing table. He saw what looked like a gun lying upon it. He stole quietly across the room. Yes it was a gun. Careless of Jameson. He picked it up and felt slightly more assured. It was a silenced weapon. But where was the girl. He was thoughtful. He concluded that she must still be at the party and would return later. Jameson must have had a few too many and returned early, was the only answer he could come up with. He moved silently into the bathroom and switched on a tiny pencil torch, shining it in the direction of the twin sinks. His eyes alighted upon their tooth-brushes neatly laid out by the chambermaid, ready for use in the morning.

Carefully he squeezed on to the two toothbrushes a powerful poison. It was colourless and easily soaked into the bristles.

However, when moisture was added, the poison would take half an hour to take effect. Long enough to get both of them. Satisfied with his work he withdrew as silently as he had arrived. Now he could deal with Coggin in his own time.

*

Normally, Jameson woke up very early each day, but today he preferred to enjoy the warmth of the bed for a longer period and so it fell to Leanna to nudge him constantly to bring him into full wakefulness. Somehow he knew he was in comfortable safety as his eyes opened reluctantly and he looked overhead at the window. Through the farmhouse window in their primitive bedroom he could see thick snowflakes descending in giant blobs.

Leanna gave up the uneven struggle.

"Stay there," she whispered. "I will go to inspect our trap," and she swung her shapely legs out of bed. Being an attractive woman she was always careful with her choice of dress, sometimes changing clothes two or even three times in a day. Today, however, she had no choice as her entire wardrobe was at the Palace Hotel. She hooked herself into her bra and gave the profile it produced a swift satisfactory look in the mirror before pulling a pale blue polo necked sweater over her head. Next she climbed into the dark blue ski pants and stooped to tug on her fur boots. She gave her face a quick application of Nivea cream and then picked up her gloves, slung her ski anorak over her arm and went.

She hummed cheerfully as she ascended in the lift of the Palace Hotel. She knew exactly what she had to do. Reaching their door she produced the torch-like object from her pocket and ran it around the door. It stayed silent. She checked the On/Off switch. Yes, it was working.

Somebody had been into their room. She opened the door six inches, and reached inside with her left hand to the time switch beside the light and switched it off. This turned off the automatic video camera they had rigged up the previous evening. Then she entered the room to examine the contents of the hidden camera which was placed just inside the doorway. Jameson had fixed the timing mechanism to switch the mechanism on when the room was entered and stay on as the subject stayed within range of the tiny camera. She examined the film through the magnified minute TV console she had brought with her for the purpose and gasped with surprise. The first sequence was of Mark Coggin entering the room, he undressed swiftly, left the Beretta gun he carried on the bedside table and went to bed. The second film began with a shot of a man's back, and then he turned, unknowingly facing the camera, to reveal the face of Senator Edward Callahan. He walked towards the sleeping figure, and paused fractionally before slipping the Beretta into his own pocket. With only a casual glance at the quilt-covered figure in the bed the mystery intruder moved into the bathroom, quietly closing the door behind him. At this point the subject had gone out of range and so the film had stopped running. The puzzled expression remained on her face. The bed had been slept in by Coggin but there was no longer any sign of him. She moved cautiously towards the bathroom where she could now hear the sound of water running. On tiptoe she moved closer and peeped through the slightly open door. At first she could see nothing until her eye reached floor level, and then she saw the spectacle of Mark Coggin in a crumpled heap on the floor. She went in. There was a horrible contorted look upon his face which left little doubt in her mind that he was dead. She stooped over him and confirmed this before sitting down on the toilet seat to think. The second intruder was not known to her but the face had a familiar look. Where had she seen it? She walked decisively back into the bedroom, picked up the telephone and asked for room service.

"We shall be spending most of today in bed," she told them curtly. "Please make sure we are not disturbed."

"Certainly, madam," replied the hotel clerk calmly.

They were used to such requests during the holiday period at the Palace Hotel.

Jameson examined the film Leanna Erhardt had handed him. From it he took two Polaroid enlarged pictures. Somehow the face in the pictures also looked familiar to him. At least Coggin hadn't taken the mystery of the identity of HH with him to the grave. Jameson reasoned the mysterious intruder could only be HH.

"You're sure he was poisoned?" he asked Leanna. "He couldn't have had a heart attack?"

"No, definitely not. He'd been cleaning his teeth and... hey, wait a minute Peter, cleaning his teeth, that's it. The poison was either on the toothbrush or perhaps in the toothpaste. And I noticed toothpaste was on both of our brushes."

"Of course," exclaimed Jameson. "Coggin confronted HH who we assume is this person here," he tapped one of the photos, "earlier in the evening. I expect he wanted a better deal than he was going to get from us. Or, even more likely, in addition to the deal he would get from us. And he told this character that I was in full possession of all the facts, as a sort of insurance policy for himself. Coggin must have thought that there was every likelihood that he himself was in danger, so knowing that we weren't in, he thought he'd be safe in our room. Ironic isn't it? He got it instead of us. That's what's known as being 'hoisted by your own petard'."

"Another of your funny English sayings?" she asked.

He nodded. "But who is he?" He pondered a moment. "I know who will know him. Come on, it's time I had a chat with Jimmy."

"Jimmy?"

"Yes, Jimmy, in the hotel pop group – Jimmy and The Raquets. I've known him for years and he knows every face in St Moritz. I think this is his fourth season!"

"No doubt at all about it, pet," said Jimmy, handing the photographs back to Jameson. "That's the brother of probably the next American President. Senator Edward Callahan. He comes here each Christmas. You want an introduction?"

Jameson shook his head dumbly. The affair was now assuming nightmare proportions. The next American President's brother!

"Hey, keep this to yourself Jim will you?" he said lightly. "I'm writing a piece for a scandal sheet, but I think this one will be too hot even for them." And then he changed the subject.

"Say, how about me compering your show one evening, like old times, and Leanna could sit in on drums, she's quite good."

"Sure Pete, let's rehearse it tomorrow. We could do with a bit of a livener in the show, got any ideas?"

Jameson now had a dilemma, as he explained to his German colleague. Knowing what he now knew he ought to telephone Commander Burt and pass the decision of what action to take to him. It was a decision of utmost responsibility and this was the Commander's job. But at the back of his mind the thought nagged Peter Jameson that Burt would have to talk to the Prime Minister who would contact the President and then diplomatic politics would take over. In all probability Senator Teddy Callahan would get away Scott free. Ronald Callahan would be eased out of the presidential race, but surely they'd have to take some action. The man had actively assisted the Russians, helped both the IRA and the Protestant extremists and been directly and indirectly responsible for the deaths of many innocent people. He'd also tried to poison Leanna and himself. With such a man at large knowing what they both knew, they could never feel totally safe. But despite the fact that he and Leanna knew Callahan was their man, the evidence was painfully thin. All he could show as evidence was two small photographs, which it could be argued, could have been taken anywhere by anyone wishing to frame the Senator. The poison could be a little tricky if the Senator's fingerprints were on the toothbrushes, but it was not conclusive evidence. He might have worn gloves. However, Jameson concluded after much mind searching and discussion with Leanna, the decision was much too big for him to take and his final argument to Leanna Erhardt was:

"I can't take the decision which could alter the history of the United States, for Christ's sake!"

So they trudged in the snowstorm to the post office to make the telephone call to Jameson's Chief in London. The call which could set the diplomatic telephones between London and Washington red hot.

"I'm sorry, sir," the post office operator informed him politely, "we have three different routes we can use out of St Moritz but the lines on all of them are down due to the storm."

"When will they be fixed?" asked Jameson.

"At least twelve hours," came the reply, "and it is still snowing, sir."

Leanna Erhardt looked at Jameson.

"It seems as if fate has taken a hand," she said. He nodded.

"Yes, the decisions have been made for us. Let's go and tackle Senator Edward Callahan. He should be waiting for this weather to lift by the Olympic jump area."

It did not occur to him to ask the girl to stay behind on what promised to be a most dangerous final chapter of the mission. She was trained for the same job as he, in fact had even more experience in the business than he had, so there was no operational reason why she should not be treated as equal. They drove back to the farmhouse to collect their skis, and Jameson sat down to write a short note of explanation to Commander Burt, just in case. Leanna examined the tiny pistol she carried on assignment and zipped it into the sleeve pocket of her ski anorak.

Jameson checked his own service weapon and strapped on the shoulder harness he so seldom used. He had little choice this time as he could hardly carry the weapon anywhere else dressed as he was in tight-fitting ski clothes.

The journey up the mountain to the Olympic ski-jumping area was cold and lonely. They were the only occupants of the

168

gondola which took them up to the first station. The only skiers today in this weather would be the jumpers and they would be waiting at the summit for the snow to abate.

"Have you made plans, Peter?" Asked Leanna as they transferred to the T Bar for the second leg of their ascent.

"Yes, I have, and I hope I'm not wrong about one or any of them. Because if I am, we could be wiped out, buried in this snow and not found until spring. You see, I think that it is highly likely that the people with Callahan will not know of his other activities. Otherwise why would he have tried to poison us himself? I can't see any other explanation. He may not know what we look like. So I'm going to, in some way, introduce myself to him. He also won't know that Coggin didn't tell me a damned thing about him."

"In other words, you're going to set yourself up as human bait?"

"Yes."

"Is that very clever?" she said sarcastically. "You might just as well have waited for the telephone lines to be repaired to achieve the same result. Except you'd stand a better chance of staying alive."

"Ah, but listen, you haven't heard the rest of my plan. So just lend me your ear. We have some evidence to create and I don't intend to let some jumped up–"

"Don't say it!"

"–kill me." Jameson finished.

They arrived at the second station and transferred to the chairlifts for the final stage of their ascent. In the stillness of that winter's afternoon, exposed as they were to the elements, Jameson now unfolded in detail the plan that had been formulating from the moment fate had dealt the card to him in the St Moritz post office casting him in the role of the avenging angel.

As the chairlift bearing Peter Jameson and Leanna Erhardt towards the peak of the Olympic jump mountain drew close to the final station, Senator Edward Callahan sat in the midst of a joyful throng of ski jumpers and spectators. There was speculation that he would do well and might even win the event. He himself felt quietly confident that with Jameson and the girl out of the way he'd be able to deal with the threat of Mark Coggin in a similar vein. Any time now Jameson's and the girl's bodies would be discovered, but as soon as their belongings were examined by the authorities, it would be very quickly realised that they were agents and the blanket of security would, as always, descend. Of course, Coggin would have to be kept out of the way, but the sleeping pill he'd planned to give him at breakfast would be as easy to administer this evening when Coggin would re-appear. He wondered why Coggin had not shown for their breakfast meeting and had not responded to his insistent telephone paging. But this did not unduly worry him. Coggin needed him. Although Coggin was a danger to him, in the long term. In the short term Coggin needed him more than he needed Coggin. Coggin had to toe the line until he got to America, and received his money and new identity. He began to feel almost cheerful as it stopped snowing and it was announced that the competition would recommence in approximately one hour. He looked out of the window at the tiny tractors flattening the landing area. He watched the steep man-made chute being prepared. The skiers, thirty-two in all, had drawn lots for position and would make two jumps each. He thrilled to the anticipation of the hundred yard dash down the speed ramp, the leap at the end of it, high in the air, the fight to maintain balance in the air, the levelling out and finally the landing on the long jumping skis. One ski would be slightly ahead of the other, and knees would be slightly bent and leaning forward to absorb the shock.

He was shaken from his dreaming by a soft voice at his elbow, saying to him quite mildly:

"I didn't appreciate your trying to poison me, Senator, and my girlfriend has decided only to clean her teeth at night from now on."

Callahan had never felt so shocked in his life. His hand flew automatically to his ski anorak pocket where he felt the comforting weight of the silenced Beretta that he had taken from Peter Jameson's room the previous night. He was pleased he had brought the weapon with him, but had only done so on impulse after Coggin had not appeared for the breakfast meeting. He had not felt a serious need for it. Now he knew he was in a tough spot, somehow Jameson had survived the poison and found out about him. This could only have been through Coggin. Had Coggin set him up? He turned to look at the serious face of Peter Jameson and knew that this was no time to bluff. Jameson knew who he was, but the Senator did not know that Jameson had almost no evidence. He said just as quietly:

"Can't we discuss this in a little more privacy?"

If Jameson had noticed the hand dart instinctively to the ski jacket pocket he gave no sign of it, saying nothing except:

"Alright, how about outside? After you."

To onlookers, it was as if the two were known to one another and were discussing nothing more serious than a ski-jump or skiing technique. They walked together away from the high altitude complex and Callahan glanced over his shoulder. There was no sign of a weapon in Jameson's hand. By now they had reached the ski lift terminal which was enclosed by a wooden shack. This was unoccupied save for the giant cogs and steel pulleys which guided the huge wire cables upon which the chairlift depended – a perfect place to die.

Out of sight the Senator's hand started to emerge from his pocket.

Jameson's hand moved swiftly towards his own bolstered weapon. Undoubtedly, his own trained draw could have beaten the clumsy attempt by Senator Edward Callahan. But as soon as he saw the silenced end of the Beretta begin to appear he knew in a flash that what he had hoped would happen, had happened.

Callahan had taken Coggin's gun as the picture he'd seen from the bedroom had shown and was using it. He let his own draw fizzle to nothing, pulling his hand back. He saw the look of triumph in Callahan's eyes. The American said:

"OK, now just keep that hand well away from that hip or you'll get it in the most painful place. Now, where's the girl?"

"Right here, Senator," said Leanna as she stepped into view from the other side of the terminal hut, her tiny gun held steadily pointing at Callahan. Callahan's finger whitened on the trigger, he was now desperate.

"If you shoot me with that," he said, "you may not kill me right off, but I'll certainly get your boyfriend with this." There was a slight pause and he continued. "Now, lower that little gun and maybe we can do a deal."

She looked at Jameson who nodded, and she lowered the gun to her side, but stayed where she was. Jameson asked:

"Now, what sort of a deal? We learned most things from Coggin, before he died."

So Coggin was the one dead. That explained Jameson's presence. The Senator could not believe his luck. All he had to do was to dispose of these two and his troubles were over.

"I'm afraid you know much too much about Senator Callahan, and my other identity, HH, Jameson," he said "to live. You can associate me with Coggin, whom I poisoned in mistake for you. No, I'm afraid..." he smiled wolfishly, "you'll have to go."

He began pulling the trigger of the gun rapidly pointing it first at Jameson and then in the direction of Leanna Erhardt. He looked stupefied as he realised that nothing had happened and that Jameson had drawn his own weapon which was now pointed straight at him.

He went on wildly, pulling the trigger until Jameson said to him:

"Tough luck, Senator, that gun's got no firing pin. I removed it some time ago," and then to Leanna Erhardt he said, "do you have the Senator's words on tape, love?"

Leanna smiled and patted the butt of her tiny gun and said sweetly to the demoralised Senator, "It may not shoot such big bullets, but it sure has a captive audience."

"You're getting quite good at repartee, Leanna," Jameson said.

The loudspeaker interrupted further conversation as it began to call the competitors to the ramp. Callahan now wore the look of a man in terrible conflict with himself.

"Will you let me do one jump? For the sake of the family?" Callahan said.

Jameson looked steadily at Callahan before he replied. Here was the man who'd twice tried to kill him, cheated, killed, ordered killings without compassion and committed probably every moral crime in the book, asking him for this favour. What a request! If he allowed it maybe it was for the best.

"You don't deserve it," he said coolly, "but maybe... OK. One jump," he said, "but no tricks, and I'm right behind you until you go. I've got all the evidence I need and you can't go anywhere."

They filed into the competitors' area and Callahan made one last try:

"You won't let me off the hook then?" he enquired desperately of Jameson. "I'll give you anything. Ten million dollars, twenty million, anything!"

Jameson shook his head.

"Not my style, luv," he said. "You go take a jump."

"EDWARD CALLAHAN" the amplified voice of the announcer intoned. "NO 13."

"Well, here we go," muttered Callahan and stepped into the jump off position.

The willing hands pushed him into starting position and he hurtled down the slope and jumped. Up, up, up, he soared, he wasn't levelling off at the peak of his leap, he turned a somersault and then plunged head long towards the landing slope like a high diver, head first, and that was how he hit the tightly compressed snow, head first.

The spectators gasped, there had rarely been such a fall. The man's neck would have broken on impact. As he hit the ground, Leanna clutched Jameson's arm and buried her face into his shoulder.

"Oh Peter, it was horrible," was all she could say.

"It was the only way. You know the evidence we had. Now we can let the higher-ups sort out what they want to say to the world. It'll be quite a sensation though. Say, by the way, it wouldn't be a bad idea to have a tape recorder in the butts of all our guns, would it? I must have a word with our Q boys when I get back. It did the trick though, didn't it? Drove him to suicide. Now I have to manufacture some more convincing evidence for Commander Burt, honey, he's no dope. Take comfort you and I will be the only ones alive to know the true story of the last ten minutes of Edward Callahan. Now I will race you to the bottom!"

She nodded. "Come on," she said. "Let's get out of here. I think we could both use stiff drinks."

"Right. But take it easy as you ski down. We don't want to break the recording or our necks!"

The acute wall of sound struck them almost with a physical impact as they entered the *Jagger stube* (Hunters Inn) of the Palace Hotel. Jimmy and the Raquets were in full sound ascendancy at the hotel's tea dance. It seemed obvious that the news of the death of one of their most respected guests was either not known or had been deliberately kept quiet, as Senator Edward Callahan was far too well-known amongst the smart set for the atmosphere not to have been affected.

Jameson acknowledged band leader Jimmy's nod in his direction and led Leanna through the throng of happy winter holidaymakers to the bar. After three of Clan Stuart's best malt whiskies in swift succession they began to feel better. After the fourth they could assess the situation rationally. Coggin was still lying dead in their bathroom, and Callahan had chosen the only way out for himself. They were the only two people in the world who knew why. It was not possible to impart this exclusive information to London because telephone communication from St Moritz to the outside world had still not been restored. Jameson was glad that he had not been forced to kill Edward Callahan himself, as had been his original plan, as he could imagine the furore that would have ensued between London and Washington at his actions had he done so, on slim and mainly circumstantial evidence, it would have been argued.

To Leanna Erhardt, Jameson said, "You realise that with Coggin dead and his documentary evidence missing, there will be one hell of a row if it is found out that we forced Callahan into suicide!"

She nodded and said, "It'll be our word against the might of the Callahan machine."

Jameson pulled a face.

"Which means..." he said, "...either we find the missing evidence or, for our own sakes, we keep quiet about our discovery that Callahan was HH. There are no witnesses! But it will mean that Callahan's got away with it."

They sipped their drinks in silence for some moments before the girl said, "I searched his room thoroughly this morning after I discovered him, but found nothing."

"And", replied Jameson, "I hardly think he would be foolish enough to keep evidence at his flat in London."

"Maybe," she said, "he had a safety deposit or post box."

Jameson looked at her thoughtfully.

"No, documentary evidence is here somewhere. Something he wrote down and sent to nearby safety. Wait a minute," he exclaimed as an idea hit him, "not a safety deposit. The post!"

It was her turn to stare at Jameson, "Of course, a letter."

"Posted to himself," mused Jameson. "But not to here, it would be far too dangerous."

"Poste Restante, St Moritz," they exclaimed in unison, the answer coming to them together.

"It is time for Coggin to return from the dead," said Jameson dreamily to the girl before him. "You stay here, I have a little job to do." And he left the girl at the table and moved towards the lift.

After waiting impatiently for a while for a lift, he abandoned the idea and bounded up the stairs two at a time. He was only slightly breathless when he arrived at his own floor and let himself into his room. The bathroom was a grisly sight with Coggin still sprawled on the floor. Rigor mortis had set in and worn off, in the process freezing the jaw wide open. Jameson returned to the bedroom and turned his attention to Coggin's jacket which was draped over a chair. He was seeking means of identification. His fingers rifled through the wallet until he came to the International Driving Licence. He checked the photograph, went to his wardrobe and returned with his fur ski helmet. Once on his head the reflection in the mirror revealed only eyes nose and mouth. "Perfect," he said aloud. Hastily locking his room door behind him, he proceeded at speed to the town's head post office and the Poste Restante counter.

"Anything for me?" he asked gruffly, proffering Coggin's driving permit.

The middle aged woman in charge of the counter scarcely looked at the picture, but went away to search through the section C in her card index. Producing the appropriate piece of paper, she compared the number with that on a bulky envelope she now took from a rack of correspondence. This she handed to Peter Jameson:

"Just this Mein Herr," she said, squinting at the time stamp, "came this morning, 9.21."

Jameson took the envelope; it was in Coggin's handwriting, addressed to himself. His lips drew back, but in a mirthless smile. He thought he knew what was in the envelope. He opened it and the smile now spread over his face. Coggin's hand had reached back from death to keep his word and provide Peter Jameson with the evidence he needed. The promise had been fulfilled, albeit unwillingly.

Chapter 18
Convention in Geneva

All government officials, when they travel, travel very first class, and Commander Douglas R Burt was no exception. 'Was the lake named after the hotel or the hotel named after the lake?' Jameson had joked idly, when he'd eventually made his first visit there, and admired its excellence, with the late unlamented Mark Coggin. The Brooks-Brothers-suited, high-powered, American presence, and the Japanese camera toters, denoted the hotel's international status as no amount of satellite advertising could. And Burt had stayed on there, in luxury, awaiting the outcome of the dangerous mission he'd sent Jameson on, one week ago, the mission that agent had completed.

"A good general stays safely out of harms way in battle," Jameson had told Burt, with tongue in cheek, before he'd set off on the mission. But now Jameson had brought with him further far-reaching problems for Burt's attention.

An unscheduled meeting between security supremo and field agent was now taking place in Commander Burt's suite at that Hotel Lake Geneva International, the luxury hotel on the western side of Lake Geneva, Switzerland. It had come about as a result of receipt by Jameson of important information from his undercover Czechoslovak lady, Anna Dubric, in London. The information, covertly acquired by Mr Churchill, was contained in the shape of two hours of mixed telephone and office conversations, America, Ireland, and London participating. This in itself was valuable evidence of espionage, but what Anna Dubric had added to it revealed a further development which was dynamite. Peter Jameson had received Anna's package Poste Restante St Moritz, at the same time as the one he intercepted from Mark Coggin. The combined contents of both missives had resulted in Leanna Erhardt being left behind in St Moritz, to ski and take care of officialdom, and sent Peter Jameson hotfooting it to his boss in Geneva, armed with plans for violent countermeasures he believed necessary to forcefully end the Irish American Factor.

Geneva Time

The sitting room in Commander Burt's suite boasted a magnificent view, a relaxing panorama of the distant mountain ranges which jaggedly bordered Lake Geneva. Burt and Peter Jameson stood on the balcony breathing the fresh clean air Switzerland boasts, and Jameson related the dramatic events which had resulted in the situation so far, to an attentive Commander Burt! However, this was not the major purpose for his unscheduled visit. The artistically striven for niceties of view were probably lost, therefore, on these two men from MI6. They were drinking coffee from workmanlike mugs as they talked, and in the Commander's room on the coffee table was a pile of miniature audio cassettes. This was in part the St Moritz evidence Burt did expect, and Anna Dubric's London information which he did not expect or even know about, and Jameson's sketchy report. Jameson walked into the room and over to this minor information mountain, and withdrew the single sheet of A4 notepaper, which was protruding noticeably in stark whiteness from the pile.

"That's taken care of the past Commander, so now to the future, which looks to be equally ominous. This," he said, "is a précis I've written about a famous London nighterie called The Beachcomber. If you'll read about it first, I'll explain its significance," Jameson said in deceptively mild tones. "When I first read Coggin's document, which remember was only meant to be his insurance policy, and not intended for my eyes, then coupled it with Anna's bombshell, I was worried witless! Mine is a radical solution," Jameson said very seriously, "it involves billions and people in very high places, we're not playing ducks and drakes."

Burt took the sheet of paper and began to read.

"The Beachcomber has been designed as a 'nighterie' by a Hollywood film studio, on Las Vegas lines. Its presence there would be in keeping with the many extravaganzas on view in the city of Vegas. But located in London, in the heart of Mayfair, it is an outstanding phenomenon. Its presence in Great Britain's capital came about this way:

"During an actor's strike, an hotel owner, who was also an American film producer, instructed his laid off film set technicians, to create for his night spot, a true Hawaiian atmosphere."

'Has Jameson gone off his rocker? Why is he writing up this place? What does he plan to do with it?' Burt thought as he read, 'Blow it up, why the detail?' But he read on.

What they came up with was a South Pacific Robinson Crusoe type island, around which was designed a lavish restaurant in London's Mayfair Hotel. What Robinson Crusoe Island has, are mountains with waterfalls, realistically lighted periodic electrical thunderstorms, with acoustics, and live baby alligators swimming in a lagoon. The rockfaces fashioned as mountains with a waterfall, sweep down from the basement's high ceilings, into a dog-legged lagoon. A balcony is a customer's make believe mountain plateau, and is built at its summit. With water constantly cascading, the effect is as realistic as only Hollywood could make it!"

"It is as impressive a place as you will find, sir, er... favoured by plebeians and the landed gentry alike," Jameson said to his boss. Burt seemed by his expression to be puzzled by the relevance of what he'd just read. "Plebs and Pseuds I believe the modern expression is," he said condescendingly. "I'm not trying to sell you the idea as a venue for the MI6

Christmas party, sir, if that crossed your mind, I wrote up the description of the place in the lobby downstairs, using two fingers on the hotel's typing machine, because I wanted you to appreciate how good the bait is. And I want us to blow part of it up together with a hard core of the ungodly to conclude this deadly Irish American Factor!"

Commander Burt looked at Peter Jameson as if his brief earlier thought had been confirmed, and an expression of incredulity engulfed his face. He said soothingly, "Jameson, did something happen to your head on the top of that Eichorn mountain? Did the rare air give you a brain storm, or merely accelerate a process already underway in the cerebellum, deep in your brain?" Burt's voice ended in a bark. He paused and without waiting for an answer went on. "Your idea for mopping up with a bang, as you put it, doesn't bear serious consideration, and sounds to me like a script for a spy picture! Not a serious proposal. What is your master plan? What are your reasons for expecting me to consider a blood bath, involving the public, in a top London hotel? And how do you intend to blow it up?" Burt said sarcastically, "Reincarnate Guy Fawkes?"

Jameson hoped he did not sound patronising when he said, "I did think I might get this reaction from you sir, so let me elucidate. There are really exceptional circumstances, of which I have only recently become aware, which will justify my seeming madness! It involves a new arms route, oil and a new terrorist link up. I haven't had time so far, or thought it wise so far, to commit all the possibilities to tape. But with bombs – don't the IRA always like to claim responsibility anyway? Remember your words to me at the cricket, Commander!" Jameson smiled now. "They won't wanna' claim this one if I get my way. I think you will appreciate the irony of The Beachcomber bang when you have heard all those reasons. I thought some of those reasons so sensitive that they should be... for your eyes only!"

"Then try me, Jameson," said Burt, "after I have listened to what you have seen fit to entrust to tape, at dinner tonight. You will never find me unresponsive to irony, young man, nor especially new ideas. But I have to say, at first hearing, I think that you may have taken leave of your senses! More coffee, Jameson... strong coffee or would you prefer a strong Scotch?"

Commander Burt now walked over to the collection of information stacked in a pile on the coffee table.

"Giving me deadlines too, are you now Jameson?" he said noting the tag hanging from the Churchillian cigar on the paper weight. This bore the words, 'St Valentine's Day'. He picked up the Churchill figurine and said, "Interesting piece of surveillance equipment, obtrusively unobtrusive and therefore bloody effective for use in high places!" Burt smiled a wimpish smile. "I wonder if I'd dare give one to Allan Dallas for Christmas?"

"Why not give him one as a St Valentine's present – which in itself would be a piece of irony would it not, sir, if you agree to my plan?" Jameson said and kept his face deceptively straight. Burt looked the benevolent figure of Winston Churchill in the eye.

"You'd go for a big bang wouldn't you?" he said sotto voce. "Because you believed in purposeful people! But then you divided Ireland," he said to Jameson. "Was this design idea yours, Jameson, or ours?"

"It was my idea sir, but Q Department's expertise. I had them make up a whole collection of politicians for the exact purpose you had in mind." Now was the time to patronise the old man, as he closed in for the kill. "We call them our Secure-a-World All Time Parliament. General De Gaulle's got his sound pick up in his honker!" he smiled. "And Churchill's got his in his cigar.

"But, wait until you hear what Winnie's got stored on that tape in his belly sir! Here's a sample. Libyan oil is breaking the embargo, provenly bought with American money (raised by Irish passion)! So how about a pirate sea venture the like of which won't have been seen since the days of Sir Francis Drake! But in the twentieth century, the yellow gold is black gold. The plan is for it to be shipped illegally using renegade Libyan tankers of similar appearance chartered from Iraq. Flag swapping takes place in the Med, and the oil is refined, factored and sold through the IRA in Ireland – on paper to American outlets. Now do I get a serious hearing to explain how I think it's done?"

Burt said, "You'll get dinner at one of Switzerland's best later, but start at the beginning – your dark suggestion for blowing up parts of a nightclub has worked on the serious side of my curiosity in line with what else you've told me," Burt smiled. "Can I blackmail you with a Scotch – Famous Grouse isn't it?"

The Mouvenpick Restaurant - Geneva

"And you want to blow this place up?" repeated Commander Burt mildly. "Er... won't this Mr Danzigger have something to say about that?"

It was now evening and the Commander's promised meal was being enjoyed at Geneva's fashionable Mouvenpick restaurant, and this laconic question was only one of many put by the Commander, as Jameson unfolded his narrative during the course of their hors d'oeuvre.

The restaurant of Burt's choice was a cheerful friendly establishment, and the boisterous, carnival atmosphere the management encouraged meant that any overhearing of what was said at Jameson and Burt's table would be of little consequence.

Jameson smiled. "He might if he still owned it," he said, "but it's just been sold." His smile became a conspiratorial one. "The place is being sold to the Japanese who intend to close it. We, masquerading as the IRA, will do it for them and achieve our purpose, and they will get the windfall of the insurance settlement!"

"Jameson you're a rogue," Burt said, "and pulling such dubious strokes of deception in the Government's name I have to say is inexcusable!"

"Deception is a deceptive word in itself Commander," countered Jameson matching his chief's judicial tones, "and constantly used by Government when it suits them, and by lawyers when they can't lay tongue to definitive twistable phrases."

"I was saying that your deception would be inexcusable but masterly," Burt said, then went on. "OK, Jameson, on your eloquence, and slightly against my better judgement, I agree we'll do it. Now you've convinced me, which means it's my turn to convince others that I'm not mad, we'll examine the 'nuts and bolts'. We need to know a lot more about Benson's operating plan if we're to intercept that first oil shipment, and who the personnel concerned are, with their local organisation connections. Can I safely leave you to liaise with Anna?" Burt said, "Brief her on a need to know basis." There was just a hint of triumph in Jameson's smile, as he nodded affirmatively and said, "What a good decision it was of yours, sir, to give Anna Dubric a break."

Jameson paused, as the well-endowed, dirndl-clad Swiss waitress busied herself about her duties bending low at their table, and he allowed his eyes to linger deep within her cleavage, before she left, and he continued.

"The Beachcomber can be hired for private functions, and Anna has hired the main part, that's like the stalls (in a theatre) lock, stock, cabaret and all, for an Irish evening there on St Valentine's Night. This was what turned my thoughts, initially, to the wicked possibilities of our caper! Although I didn't know it then, the powerful Mrs McGuinness will be there, with four faceless IRA Council Members! And Messrs Sweeney and O'Hara too, amongst many we don't have proper information on. So if ever the devil could cast his net guv..." Jameson inclined his head.

Burt stirred his coffee more fiercely than before, as he replied, "A big operation's launch it would seem. The oil and arms development launch at a guess, I could seriously work with that figuration. Yes, I go along with it. We will never have a better chance Jameson," Burt said. "And I can now take your point about wrapping up the Irish American thing with a big bang and not too many questions that would embarrass the Americans being asked!" Burt was now more than enthusiastic, "Dallas will love me for that one and be happy to provide the shipping! Why didn't you tell all this before?"

"I only made contact with Anna personally when I phoned her this afternoon, so how could I sir? But I trust now that I have, it's improved the taste of your asparagus, and now do ya' cop the irony I promised you? An IRA St Valentine's Day Massacre, not a Guy Fawkes Gunpowder Plot, in which we will execute all our *persona non grata*, Chicago mobsters and others, and leave the IRA's calling card!"

Commander Burt's attitude was brusque as he hammered out details with Peter Jameson.

"So you supervise her exit just before the bang, and you make sure no one important gets away. No prisoners!" Burt said emphatically. "You know what that means!"

Jameson nodded. Burt meant the death sentence.

"What those bastards had in mind for the Royals, and that much we do have, with recognisable voices, on tape as evidence, very much swayed me in the yes direction before this development. Now I will personally arrange the coded message, from the IRA to MI5, with my opposite number. But the warning will be one minute only, before the SAS begin their sortie. Our timing has to be spot on as I don't want the emergency services being caught in any cross fire... and the press must never get even a sniff that this was not genuinely the work of the IRA. American warships are always sniffing around oil tankers in that region of the Med, so that part of the eventual operation will not be deemed particularly suspicious.

Chapter 19

A Deadly Destination

"I invited you here to the Royal Borough of Kensington, Anna, for me to receive a verbal report from you, and for me to brief you on how you are to fit into a very dangerous operation. Instead of which, I have ended up bowing to your female charms and getting side tracked into a sauna and bedroom scene," Jameson said, putting on a show of pique.

This conversation was taking place in Jameson's Knightsbridge apartment as he and Anna Dubric relaxed on the sitting room floor clad in fluffy white bath robes, in preparation for the steam.

"Very unprofessional of me to be sure. But I have been very busy since I got back from Geneva, and it has been a long time between drinks!"

"Liar, darling," countered a dreamy Czechoslovak lady. "Peter Jameson always finds nooky time, and he knows exactly what he's doing," a meaningful smile accompanied her statement. "But instruct on, sir!" She said.

Her tone, although bantering, hid a very attentive and naturally perceptive attitude just beneath the surface. Jameson had good reason to know this, and Anna knew her life could depend on more than the odd pleasant bedroom scene played out with this Special Branch field agent. But Anna Dubric's most valuable asset was that she was all woman, easy on the eye, and at the intriguing age of on the green side of thirty and she knew that.

"The man you know as Shaheen, is Shaheen El Baag, Abdul must be his nightclub name," Jameson said. "The stuff I got from Coggin hinted at what was afoot, although it didn't detail anything definite, it did tell us how the oil swindle was to work. The stuff you sent me neatly spelt it out. This proves, I think, that the fact of HH's death is not widely known yet amongst the ungodly, but that the organisation continues. So be very careful you don't slip up." The girl nodded her head, understanding. Jameson continued, "Since we've known who he is, Shaheen has been under observation since he arrived in this country from Munich where he has residency, together with about every known spy you can think of, including me," Jameson grinned. "It must have scared the proverbial pants off you meeting a client under such circumstances, a nightclub hostess's dread!" 'Bastard,' thought Dubric, 'I'll get him when he's asleep,' and remained silent. "But his appearance is particularly worrying."

"Why?" she asked curiously. "Isn't he just another terrorist arms supplier using the Beauvais, Lydd, Irish route?"

"No, I don't think so, although probably that's where the original connection was. Because he's a route provider you see. He's the one putting the oil route swindle together and this necessitates payment in laundered money. But we're on to that one. What worries me is the possibility of terrorist swapping. I think we see the beginnings of a merger in terrorist organisations, amongst other things. Commander Burt has said to me more than once that it would be disastrous if it ever happened," Jameson went on. "The HH outfit has the contacts worldwide to provide the organisational network including suppliers, and the IRA and Middle East terrorists need, and have the type of dedicated foot soldiers to operate, a personnel exchange!"

"You mean Arabs carrying out Irish terrorism and vice versa?" Dubric sounded sceptical. "I can see some advantages, the confusion and so on, but does it justify such a

high power arrangement when the religious reasons differ so
widely?"

"Oh yes, it does for both sides, and religion is more than
ever becoming the excuse and not the reason, as increasingly
world power politics get involved and world opinion changes.
The Muslim's avowed intention is to be the world power base
by the year 2008. They say it is written in the Koran.

"But to more immediate concerns. For instance it's now
getting difficult even for IRA people to carry out their atrocities
and run back to hide in Ireland as safely as they did! And Syria
or Libya or Algeria or any favourable Muslim country would
be excellent alternative havens would they not? And suit the
Muslim and Irish purposes. In the reverse situation, robed
Arabs are so commonplace in both Ireland and here, as to be
like hiding a Santa Claus in a field full of Father Christmas's!
Remember the Israeli Embassy bombing a while back? There
were so many Arabs around Harrods that it was impossible to
tell Peter from Paul, or Paul from Mary. Do you get those
disguise advantages? Nuns, female Arab monks..." he trailed
off. "Get it? Now can you understand how important the big
wipe out at The Beachcomber is going to be?"

Anna Dubric said humbly, "Yes I am beginning to see what
you mean, and well thought out Peter and Douglas. And yes,
he told me when he danced with me at the club to call him that
off duty!"

"Bloody 'ell," Jameson said. "Even I'm not allowed that!"

"No, I'm just a small cog in the wheel who needs to play
her part and keep her head down. But you said you had to
brief me on my involvement." She sat up alertly, perfecting an
all revealing sit up. "Now then, the Beachcomber party, are
you going to tell me about the raid?"

"It's not going to be a raid the way you might think Anna,
it's gonna' be a bombing commando raid! We are going to
bomb it."

"You are what?" gasped Dubric. "Why? Surely a simple
raid by the SAS..." she trailed off.

Jameson said, "No, SAS squads don't work that way, and we looked at the standard raiding option, and discarded it for a variety of reasons. Lots of 'em legal, which your Douglas constantly reminds me of, and others, but they needn't concern you. But I can tell you I had to do battle royal with the old man to get him to agree to do it any way! Now... The Beachcomber evening is to be a private party with fancy dress masks, for between eighty and a hundred people occupying the ground floor of the basement right?" Jameson grinned, "That description sounds Irish in itself doesn't it, ground floor occupying the basement?" Dubric nodded affirmatively. "The plateau first floor will be open to the public, that suits our purpose but requires ace care for the public on our part. The rank and file to provide their own face masks, and you to provide the top table's right?" The girl nodded again. Jameson went on, "That is what we reckon because about seven out of those top ten faces, six if you don't include Shaheen, will be unknowns, and we'd dearly like to know unofficially who they are, but it suits us not to really! So their identities will be hidden behind custom-made masks. This plays nicely into our hands because we can pinpoint them more easily."

The girl nodded and smiled. "Understood," she said. "And I'm not completely dim Jamesy! Let me guess. You want duplicates made of those masks so that the SAS assassinate the correct people, right?"

Jameson looked surprised. "Right," he replied. "How did you guess?"

Not realising Jameson was leg pulling Anna said, "Guess Peter, huh, it was as easy as tweaking your third leg! You almost spelt it out to me in the first line when you implied that the SAS do not do non-killing raids, and then you crossed the t's and dotted the i's for me when you told me the SAS needed to be able to pick the ungodly out from the crowd, when you zoomed in on the need to recognise the top ten! What I haven't quite been able to work out is how I avoid getting blown up in the process. I, you may have noticed, am not built like a commando, Jameson. But now I am a little tired and didn't you say ages ago that it's been a long time between drinks!"

She rose from the floor and allowed her robe to fall gracefully from her shoulders and then to the floor as she stretched. She ruffled her blonde hair, cupped both breasts in her hands and artistically massaged them in gentle, sexy, circular movements. Then provocatively she uplifted them, watching Jameson's passions stirring, and smiled. "Where to big boy?" She said in husky tones. Jameson wolf whistled, and stroked her body imaginatively, before his face sought the haven of a generous acreage.

Breakfast at Jameson's

"And now let me tell you something else my Big Annie," Jameson was talking as the two breakfasted the following morning. "I was not kidding you in the least when I said I'd been busy since I got back from Geneva! I've been very busy indeed! Like training intensively with the SAS, planning the assault on The Beachcomber, on an assault course in Norfolk! And even getting my feet wet on another part of the plot which doesn't concern you. We've planned and rehearsed, and rehearsed and planned the operation like an action feature film."

"Really," commented a now fully-dressed Anna, curling one lip over her coffee cup. I have to look after your exit, and make sure we take no political prisoners. I believe the IRA consider themselves an army, therefore the Geneva Convention allows for executions for those on enemy territory out of uniform as spies. So I have no problems with conscience or legality. And we will blame the action on the IRA, and confusion will reign."

Anna Dubric thought Peter Jameson looked very pleased at this prospect.

"Talking of executions and spies and confusion. Will you be wearing a duplicate mask?" she asked.

"Yes, I've decided on St Christopher, the patron saint of travel," replied Jameson.

"Well then," she said quizzically, "you will need all St Christopher's luck travelling with you on St Valentine's Night, because that's the mask chosen by O'Hara, and he's pretty fat and you're pretty thin. Tweedle Dee and Tweedle Dum?" Dubric raised her eyebrows. "You could be executed by your own people or the ungodly as you call them!"

"The fact had not escaped me honey," Jameson said, "so I shall be watching my tail better than a raw naval recruit!"

In reply Anna Dubric once more curled her lip at Peter Jameson over her coffee cup. This gesture Jameson ignored but said, "Now pay attention lady, this is your only briefing." He picked up his pencil and opened a large sketch pad.

The End for Anna

"At 22.00 hours six SAS commandos will burst on to this plateau balcony area above the waterfall here," Peter Jameson indicated the area on the large sketch pad, which he drew on as he spoke. He traced the balcony area. "It is similar in size I suppose to that of the mezzanine in a small cinema, where this night club has six tables set up, or about forty covers I suppose," he said.

"But isn't that the only section which will be open to the general public that night?" Dubric said questioningly.

"I know that, but listen please! The SAS men will wear black track suits and balaclavas, and be armed with specially adapted single shot, rapid shot, and gas shot, machine pistols. They will all be wearing gas masks, and one man only will be left to cover any diners and deal with any would be heroes. He will use the gas only status on his weapon, which will be on and used in an *emergency only*. The gas he uses will be temporarily disabling, but otherwise harmless in the long term, satisfied?" Jameson asked. "Because they will be taking blame, we want members of the public to believe our men are members of the

IRA! The remaining five, one is a woman Anna, your stand in at rehearsals, will hurl a mixture of high explosive hand grenades, and very strong tear gas grenades below, into the stalls (the main restaurant), in and around the top table, and the showtime stage, about thirty feet below. During the maximum general panic created the raiding commandos will, using grappling irons and ropes, shin down, and enter the dining area through the waterfall. They will make straight for the top table, confront and execute those who have survived the grenade attack and who resist, then attempt to identify using ID cameras, clear up and leave. The whole job takes under fifteen minutes, because we've got less than that, from start to a comb out," Jameson finished.

"The way you tell it, Peter, makes it sound like a stroll," Dubric said. "Just another day's work for a highly trained team at rehearsals – but are you really sure it's gonna' be alright on the night?" she asked.

"Like all good plans this one relies on simplicity, timing, and surprise, my dear!" Jameson said. "Complicated plans usually produce complicated cock-ups! I was there and worked with these people in routine practice – that part of the operation will work!" Jameson said convincingly.

As he talked Jameson still sketched, and Anna Dubric could see that he was drawing the ground floor (deep basement area) elevation of The Beachcomber. "This is the main dining and entertainment area, and here's the stage at the opposite end to the waterfall," said Jameson indicating with his pencil, "and through here," his pencil sketched in an archway, "is the off restaurant entrée bar, where you will be sitting, facing the main entrance. I too will get in there and mingle, at some time shortly before the action starts. We will be able to see through the open trellis work here." Jameson's pencil drew a thin straight line from the bar to the top of the waterfall, artistically. "Now then, the electrical thunder storms, which are dramatic flashes of forked lightening licking across scudding black clouds in the sky, with accompanying sounds of thunder, are on a time switch which operates automatically every twenty minutes. So at the first clap of thunder at 22.00 hours you put this on." Jameson reached under the table in his table where the two still sat, to produce a sports holdall. From it he extracted a Mickey Mouse mask, and Dubric could see it had behind it the workings of an artfully concealed miniature gas mask. Wryly Anna's thoughts went to Disneyland and fantasy, from which this situation was not too far removed. "You put this on at the sound of the first thunder clap and then you take your cue from me!" Jameson said. "Any questions?"

'B' Day At The Mayfair

Peter Jameson was talking with Commander Douglas Burt in the Edward Danzigger suite at The Mayfair Hotel, from where his part in Operation B Day would start later that evening.

"It seems the IRA Security Council have organised their own security measures to make sure their unknown faces stay unknown, sir," Jameson said. Burt raised a questioning eyebrow.

"A DHL security collection van arrived unannounced with a written collection order late yesterday. Its stated orders were to collect six fancy dress masks and deliver them air to air to Shannon Airport, Ireland. The information Anna was able to glean from the driver was that their final destination was to an unspecified drop box at Shannon. So in no way now will it be possible to know in advance who those top six are – but that's no big thing Commander!"

Burt was brusque in reply. "It might mean some faces behind the masks are found to be Irish American, and this security smacks distinctly of the American style!" Burt said tersely. "But it does substantiate Coggin's written revelations of the planned illegal oil route from Libya, and justifies the marine blockade caper we've planned."

"Security!" Jameson suddenly exclaimed. "Why didn't I put two and two together before Commander?"

Burt frowned. "What do you mean Jameson, security?"

Jameson said, "We've found out, Mark Coggin told me and even put it in writing, that Callahan religiously kept up and used his Yale fraternity connection, and that some classroom friends later went on to constitute his personal security, right? Yale is like all American universities, it has to have an excellent College Football Team, it's a status symbol, and American football players are very big men, that seems to be a requirement of their national game too," Jameson went on. "And Coggin's written description in the document you've just referred to Commander, of the bodyguard who killed our good friend Inspector Fisher, was: He was a mountain of a man!"

"Time will tell if you're right Jameson, and right I believe you might just be!" Burt said thoughtfully. "But to the business tonight. I have arranged that the coded IRA warning will be made to Scotland Yard two minutes before actual proceedings begin, and MI5 will manoeuvre the emergency services so as to be at The Beachcomber thirteen minutes after that." Burt fixed on Jameson, what Peter Jameson later described as his ancient mariner's look. "Your people must leave in the confusion as the official cavalry arrives, so you have no more than fifteen minutes to get in... do the job... and get out. Remember my admonition to you young man, about political prisoners! If you fail me Jameson, I shall have you hanging from the proverbial yardarm! But if you satisfy me I shall reward you with the job of your dreams."

Beachbaby-Beachbaby

Peter Jameson had made his plans carefully as to how to effect his entry, as the uninvited guest at the private Valentine's party. He was immaculately clad in a dinner jacket, which featured a Gaelic bow tie for SAS recognition, and he had drawn upon boyhood experiences as to how to get in free to cinemas, as his adult method of gaining unnoticed entrance to The Beachcomber and this was via the gentlemen's lavatory.

His reconnoitre of The Mayfair Hotel had earlier revealed that there was an openable skylight, directly above The Beachcomber's men's conveniences area. 'This will be my point of entry,' thought Jameson. 'I will hang from the window ledge and drop the ten feet and make a spectacular entrance to an audience of cheering white porcelain urinals! Nobody asks you for your ticket when you walk out of the gent's loo,' he chucklingly told himself. All key Beachcomber staff at the sharp end of the evening's enterprise were covered by discreet substitutions, using either Special Branch or SAS personnel, and Jameson made a mental note to apply for Equity Memberships for the latter when they left military service, so versatile were they already in terms of their acting capabilities.

Peter Jameson checked the action on his Walther PPK automatic pistol, which contrary to rumour did not jam unless used by its operator like a machine gun. Satisfied, he snapped into its butt a full customised clip of ammunition, sixteen rounds in all. His dinner jacket had been specially cut to accommodate the weapon, the bulge it made, therefore, was not more than that of a well-filled wallet. The Walther's silencer he stowed elsewhere because the six extra inches made for a cumbersome draw in emergencies, and for a distinct lack of mobility when indulging in break-ins! But it looks good in movies, Jameson granted. Into his pockets, right and left, were placed two, strong mix, tear gas grenades and other unspecified specialities were divided about his person. His St Christopher gas mask he carried in his hand. He was ready to do battle.

Jameson left the Danzigger Suite located on the fourth floor, covertly via the bathroom window, and descended the iron fire escape steps, until he reached the skylight window of The Beachcomber's gentlemen's washroom. Looking through it, it appeared to Jameson that his luck was in, as nobody was in visible occupation. But luck being in depended upon your view, which was brief for this intruder. As Jameson was dropping in, the entrance door to the gentlemen's toilet was opening, and a man walked in to observe all. To Jameson, as he landed, this was a huge man at first sight, from toes up, to Jameson he seemed ten feet tall! However, he was probably a shade under six ten! The huge man moved towards Jameson menacingly, who stayed crouched in his landing position. Like a heavy weight boxer preparing a crushing knock out punch, which was undoubtedly the intention of the man, he drew back his right arm in telegraphed slow motion, for the haymaker punch. Slow pace and Jameson's speed and wit then took a hand against him, the three seconds the winding up took accounted for the difference between living and dying as the man mountain ran into a terrific uppercut from Jameson. This punch started from the floor, where Jameson crouched, but it had the recoil of Jameson's landing impetus, and the thrust of nearly fourteen stones of solid bone and muscle, plus the specialised knowledge of the precise spot on the man's temple where the blow would be fatal! This was Fisher's killer who'd just walked in, and that was what went through Jameson's mind as he delivered the killer blow, which is taught to but a few field agents in Special Branch's MI6. Time and speed was now of the essence because 22.00 was fast approaching, and a dead giant on the gent's floor might be explainable – but only just! Jameson grasped the dead man by both wrists and hauled him into the nearest cubicle backwards, then set about the difficult manoeuvre of sitting him on the lavatory seat. This successfully done he went through the man's pockets. It was the American passport which gave Jameson most satisfaction. The man's name was Joseph Delemar Kennedy, and in his passport there was an entry visa to the UK which was stamped Yeadon Airport, West Yorkshire. Jameson smiled grimly and said out loud, "Well I got the man who got you Fish, and I did it the way you'd have approved of most – man to man." With a special little instrument attached to a special Special Branch pen, Jameson was able to lock the WC door from the outside. Mr Kennedy would not be disturbed, and with the time at ten minutes before 22.00 Jameson put on his St Christopher mask and made his way through the restaurant, and into the entrée bar, aptly named the Hawaii Five O.

Waiting and the use of time thereof, is part of a Special Branch field agent's training, and Jameson used his to good purpose to assess the traffic circulating in The Five O Bar. It seemed to be constant, with little to-ing and fro-ing and this was perfect for the operation's purpose. There were between twenty-five and thirty people seated, and a group of 'hard core men at the bar' drinkers, standing around it. Only about half wore their masks, and those who did were mainly the women. Jameson kept his at hand on the table where he sat alone, as, he noted from a casual glance, did Anna. When the action started he would, he planned, roll his gas grenades strategically, put his mask on and take up position by the restaurant's entrance arch. From there he would fulfil his 'no political prisoners to be taken' role. This meant none of the top table to survive. He could see Anna Dubric held her Mickey Mouse mask firmly in her hand, and her gaze was never far from the balcony skyline where the action would commence.

At the first clap of thunder Jameson went into action as planned and the unobtrusive despatch of his grenades went unnoticed as he actioned them. However, the war whoops of the SAS in action within split seconds, coincided with the growing pandemonium of a stunned audience, no doubt believing this to be part of the show's entertainment, until the gas began to take effect and realisation dawned, it was not!

From the moment Peter Jameson had walked through the wide arched entrance from the restaurant into the Five O Bar, Anna Dubric, whose table was positioned there as a sponsor's representative, had alternated her gaze about equally between the restaurant's plateau and his table. A good five minutes had now passed since the operation began, hand grenade explosions had rent the air, and tear gas made vision resemble an old fashioned foggy day in London town. She'd lost sight of Jameson and had seriously begun to wonder about his instruction to her to sit tight and take her cue from him!

Suddenly he appeared beside her openly screwing a silencer onto a handgun.

"Three minutes to go Anna," he said, "and I'll be back for you. We may not have arrived together but we will leave together, and the SAS only know where you are if you stay where you are."

Jameson had been aware as soon as the bomb attack began that should any of the top ten survive, particularly O'Hara or Sweeney, they would target Anna as the betrayer. But the SAS operation had gone according to plan. On and around the top table was a huddle of injured or dead bodies. As Jameson watched from his vantage point an SAS person clinically examined the masked, still figures in the carnage for identification, whilst another looked on.

But one was getting away, Jameson now observed, because disappearing behind the curtain of The Beachcomber stage was one fat Joe O'Hara. Jameson moved in for the kill, no political prisoners Burt had said, and crept stealthily into the wings. Cautiously, gun in hand Jameson focused one eye, the rest of him under cover, in the direction of the stage wings entrance opposite to him. The footlights he could see were casting an eerie shadow, a silhouette, as caricatured Hitchcock in the old TV series, on a rotund figure opposite. It was O'Hara who was frantically wrestling with the door handle and trying to escape through the locked stage door exit. Jameson knew it was locked because he had locked it earlier and it was his planned route of departure. Jameson carefully aimed with the Walther, took up first pressure, and squeezed the trigger, twice.

Anna Dubric was surprised and very relieved, when Jameson emerged like a will o' the wisp from nowhere, to appear by her side and say, unhurriedly, "Come along Cinderella it's time to leave this ball." He took her hand and they retraced his steps quickly to the stage and the stage door. Jameson opened it with his 'all-purpose pen', they stepped over O'Hara's body and went down a short flight of stairs, which led through yet another door, and they ran into a long straight passage. "This leads to the old Colony Restaurant," explained Jameson, "and comes out at the bottom of Berkeley Square, where your coach of white mice and liveried chauffeur, in the shape of Commander Burt's car and driver, awaits you!"

"How you can joke in times like this Peter..." she panted.

"Oh I'm not joking luv - you'll see," replied a mysterious Jameson. True to his word and the plans, Wilkes was waiting by a black limousine in which the pair deposited themselves. Jameson looked at his watch and treated Anna Dubric to a satisfied smile.

"There you are Anna, I told you the whole job would take under fifteen minutes from start to comb out! It's just about that now, and... just about now, MI5 will be starting to comb out!"

"I'm impressed but..."

"You will continue to be I hope. Er, Arthur," he called to Wilkes, who was driving efficiently fast, "how long to Heathrow?"

Rapidly recovering her composure, Anna said, "I told you I was impressed didn't I? I always knew you were not just a good fuck!"

A startled Wilkes coughed discreetly, and closed the chauffeur's partition. Jameson laughed.

They travelled in silence and in thought for some time, Anna Dubric's were ones of misgiving. Her role in all that had happened was now over she reasoned, and the British Government, wishing to be rid of embarrassment, intended to ship her swiftly abroad. The question was where? And who would believe any story she could tell? The Beachcomber affair had been manufactured to seem like an IRA atrocity gone wrong, and the ring of menace she had been hired to infiltrate was now vanquished, with its perpetrators dead. And she had not even been paid yet! Everything very neat with Jameson to see she got on the right plane! As if on cue Wilkes slid open the communicating window and said, "I was asked by

Commander Burt to hand this to you, madam." He held in his hand a bulky brown envelope.

'This is it!' Thought Anna as she took it wordlessly. 'Payment from a slush fund.' Anna Dubric continued to sit in silence with her package unopened. She would not, she thought, give this good fuck Jameson the satisfaction of seeing 'Judas count the thirty pieces of silver.' Jameson watcher her finger the package.

"Don't you want to know what's in it?" he asked, "or where you're going?"

"I think I can guess," Dubric replied in a dull voice.

"Oh," said Jameson. "I am sure you can't so I will tell you. There are plane tickets, passports, money, an itinerary and related documents. One British passport is for you and one is for your mother, who you will be meeting at Brown's Hotel, in Vienna, where you will be waiting for her. She does not know why she is presently being kept awaiting documentation at the British Consulate, and she doesn't know that you are coming."

"Jameson!" cried Anna Dubric hoarsely. "When I said you were a good fuck Jamesy – I should have said you are a fucking good fuck! This is the best news you could ever give me!"

Wilkes was coughing discreetly again, and closed his communications window.

Diplomatic VIP Lounge - Heathrow

"Now is the time for all good men to come to the aid of the party," said Commander Burt dryly to Jameson, as he strode in, later than scheduled, to the VIP lounge at London's Heathrow, to greet his welcoming party. "I take it everything went satisfactorily with Anna Dubric!"

"Yes sir, I left her still shell-shocked in the duty frees, and trying, metaphorically speaking, to pinch herself. She hasn't seen her mother in nearly a decade!" Jameson explained.

"Good!" said Burt. "It's satisfying to play fairy godmother, and plucking suspicious people from behind even crumbled Iron

Curtains, for one of this country's illegal immigrants, is still difficult."

"We owe her too," Allan Dallas the lean, grey, moustachioed CIA chief, interjected. "One of those assassinated IRA Council Members was also an American Fund Raising Senator don't forget, who had a $1,000,000 cheque payable to Benson Arms Sales International, in his wallet!"

"Let me guess, Allan," said Jameson, "he went to Yale too!"

"This is a very unofficial meeting," Burt said, "so I can tell you what MI5 have told me, and we can tell the Prime Minister what we think he should hear, when we meet him at number ten on Wednesday."

"That'll suit me," Dallas said, "because I can endorse what we agreed with the President at Regents Park (the American Ambassador's residence) tonight. I won't have to face your PM but our President won't dare to disagree when I tell him that the renegade senator was a Democrat!"

Chapter 20

Bombshell From Downing Street

Leanna Erhardt sat with Peter Jameson in the black London taxi cab; they were on their way to visit the British Prime Minister at No 10 Downing Street. Her feelings were very mixed. This was only her third visit to London and the city still rather overwhelmed her. But now she was only minutes away from meeting Britain's most important figurehead.

The taxi moved around Trafalgar Square and entered Whitehall as Leanna Erhardt's thoughts continued. Prior to the unexpected meeting at Heathrow, she had been amazed that she was to be included in such an important meeting with no less a person than the British Prime Minister, but many questions had been asked and answered. They were now only minutes away from their destination and she was more nervous now than she had been on the Eichorn when she'd wondered if it was to be her gun which would spit the bullets to end Callahan's life.

The policeman guarding the entrance to No 10 smiled at them both after scrutiny of Jameson's security pass, and gave a coded knock upon the famous door which was opened for them. The alert-looking security officer had been expecting them.

"Morning, Mr Jameson, madam," he said, and consulting his watch, "you're a bit early. You're expected at 10.30. If you'd like to sit here," he indicated a recess where chairs surrounded a Queen Anne table, "I'll get you some coffee."

After they were seated Leanna Erhardt eyed the surroundings. What style and dignity this house had. It was the sort of place girls dreamt about. She felt somebody in this place. Jameson interrupted her thoughts.

"If Kissinger can't become President of the United States, what chance do you think you've got as Prime Minister of the UK?" he said, a touch of his old humour returning. Before she could give him a suitable reply the grey flannelled detective returned to usher them into the morning room.

"It's not just the enormity of the mission you have so successfully accomplished," said the Prime Minister after the exchange of introductions, "but also the skilful diplomacy you have shown which, from your record, would not have appeared to be a natural gift."

What crap had Burt and Dallas blown the afternoon before they'd got to this rehearsed meeting, wondered Jameson?

Jameson effected an outward smile, which to him felt like a foolish grin, and inwardly thought 'here we go with the politicians routine'. He wondered what details concerning him had been given to the PM to provoke that remark. In addition to himself and Leanna Erhardt, in the PM's office were Commander Burt and another man who, they discovered, was the personal aide of the American President, flown in specially for the occasion.

"Jameson never stops surprising me, Prime Minister," spoke up Commander Burt, coming to Jameson's aid.

"Well, of course, so it seems," said the Prime Minister easily, "and his efforts appear to have been somewhat summary."

"Very necessary, sir, in the circumstances," replied the Commander quickly.

"I think it was the best course of action. Quite clever I believe. It saved a lot of embarrassment," he addressed his last remark to the American aide, who nodded acquiescence.

"It never ceases to amaze me how your Government can get things done with such speed. Thirty-six hours after I've spoken with your President, you're here in my office with a personal letter from him."

"Well, yes, sir, Mr Prime Minister. I guess he felt that's the way he had to handle things, and I reckon he's god-damned grateful to you all here, and you too, ma'am, and a mite embarrassed too." Looking towards the girl and Jameson, the PM then continued.

"I'm going to take the unprecedented action of allowing you to read this letter addressed to me from the President of the United States. I say unprecedented, because such a document is usually seen only by members of the Cabinet and myself, but you'll hear why later."

He passed the letter, which had been the only piece of paper on the PM's otherwise empty desk, Jameson had noticed it when he'd seated himself upon entering the PM's office. He opened the envelope and withdrew the document. It was headed 'The President of the United States of America, the White House, Washington DC' and it read:

Dear Mr Prime Minister,

Your news over the hot-line shocked me deeply and you have my word as the President of this great nation that the organisation left behind by the late Senator Edward Callahan will be pursued relentlessly by personally assigned officers of my law enforcement agencies.

It augurs well for the special relationship that has existed for the last two centuries between our great nations. I am deeply indebted to you in as much as one of your brave agents constantly risked his own life in order to remove this scourge from our society. I feel no useful purpose would be served to reveal publicly the true nature of Callahan's activities; I feel it would cause panic in the money world and would almost certainly be used to our disadvantage by our enemies.

I hope to arrange through diplomatic channels in the next one to two months an official Presidential visit to your country and this will be stated officially as a visit to discuss a large financial grant from the International Monetary Fund. However, in reality, you may rest assured that every last cent our accountants figure that Senator Callahan embezzled from the United Kingdom will be repaid in full by the United States of America. My congratulations, sir, on the magnificent effort your country made in the field of intelligence and counter-espionage and my further congratulations to the agent who acted with such bravery, fortitude and diplomacy in this matter. I hope I may have the opportunity of meeting him in the United States in the near future. Due to the high security coding of this message it will be delivered to you by my own personal aide, Frank Dumme).

Our thanks to your nation, Mr Prime Minister.

President of the United States of America.

Jameson read the letter, noting the President's easily legible signature and noting from it that he was left-handed.

Leanna Erhardt read it over his shoulder, after glancing enquiringly at the Prime Minister who'd nodded his agreement. After reading the letter twice, Jameson handed it back to the Prime Minister, who placed the document in his desk drawer.

"Mr Jameson," he said, "I am going to take an action similar to the President's which will be considered by purists to be diplomatically impossible. But I believe diplomacy is changing, and the sooner we wake up to that fact the sooner we will stop dragging our feet and get back to the business of putting the great back into Great Britain. I'm asking you as a non-diplomat to deliver my reply to the President of the United States!"

"Me?"

The PM nodded and continued, "He said he wants to meet you." The PM's eyes twinkled. "You'll need to learn about 'below the line' methods, the peculiar meanings read into certain phrases, in politics as in advertising," he said.

"I shall be very heavily criticised in my Cabinet, particularly by some of the old fogies that I have to keep there to pacify the party."

Jameson spoke to the American, Frank Dumme.

"You see," he said, "sometimes even our Government gets things done!"

"Of all people," continued the PM, "Jameson has earned this honour."

A bit sugary thought Jameson, but the remark was not addressed to him. This remark he addressed to Commander Burt who had a mischievous twinkle in his eyes as he replied:

"You could argue, sir, that to send anybody else could be construed as a breach of security?"

"Oh, one more thing, Jameson. Have you ever considered going into politics?" asked the PM. He shot the question at Jameson as such an aside that it took him completely by surprise. But he replied:

"You don't know my views on politics, sir, and they are not always quite in line with yours," he said. "I find the whole scene such a charade that I would prefer not to be part of it. But under the provisions made in The Official Secrets Act, I'm duty bound to act upon what is decided to my own best judgement, Mr Prime Minister, sir."

"That's a pity, because I've been thinking of creating a new Cabinet post ever since I became PM. But looking around my own front-line I cannot find anybody who I consider would be capable, you seem a good choice."

"But you don't even know if I support your party!" said Jameson.

"You'd be surprised at what I know about you young man and the people in all the parties who are not true exponents of their own beliefs, or those of their constituents. It's impossible to know with the present three-line whip system." He pointed to his statue on the PM's desk. "Look at Churchill." Jameson smiled inwardly and wondered if Burt had told the PM the part the statue had played before presenting it as a Special Branch souvenir of technological achievement. "Probably the greatest liberal ever to become a Tory Prime Minister."

Jameson began to understand why this PM had survived in the political jungle when all the pundits had written him off as a good deputy but not tough enough for the top post. The man had the rare gift of eloquence and persuasion at all levels.

"Take TV," he went on.

"Ah, now you're into a subject I know, sir," said Jameson.

"It's dreadful. TV planners convince themselves, and only themselves, that the programmes they show are what the viewers want, and in reality they've usually got four channels all offering home-grown rubbish. And that rubbish gets 'hard sold' to the public by their own media for days. Like the old-fashioned trailers at the pictures. You know the stuff – 'Coming Shortly!' and 'All Next Week!' and 'Sunday for One Day Only!', 'Don't Miss It!' and they make even those programmes run late as a consequence. And when it comes, thinking people wonder what all the fuss was about. But lots don't switch off because they don't know it isn't worth watching until they've watched it. And they call that the ratings."

He turned to the American and said, "With respect, it's just the film moguls doing enormous deals with each other in the US and here to dump shoddy goods on both of our markets, and in the process making enormous profits for themselves."

The American responded. "Don't blame me brother. I just came to deliver a letter. I'm only the postman," he said, holding up his hands in mock defence.

"Well, it's true," Jameson addressed the PM. "It's just the same as manufacturers making shoddy goods for delivery to the public for free, and then claiming money for them, either from the Government via a TV licence or from commercial companies via highly priced advertising revenue. Then they have the cheek to brainwash us into thinking the rubbish is good. It's nothing but a Hans Christian Anderson situation and sooner or later somebody is going to say 'The Emperor's got no clothes on!'"

The PM's eyes twinkled as he listened.

"Exactly," said the PM. "That person is me. The post I had in mind for you was that of Minister of Entertainment with particular responsibility for TV and Radio Broadcasting. Still not interested?"

The atmosphere in that room was suddenly electrifying. Even the two foreigners, Leanna Erhardt and Frank Dumme, could see the brilliant political triumph this unassuming PM had perpetrated. Because there was no doubt after what he'd just said that Jameson would accept this post. Ever since the inception of radio and TV, political parties had tried untiringly to control this media and with only a modicum of, usually only temporary, success. This had to be the political stroke of the century on the home front, with the card played delicately in an atmosphere of an affair which would, if known to people outside of the PM's room, be hailed as the PM's coup of the century. Commander Burt spoke.

"It will be a beautiful cover for me when I need him too, sir. Peter Jameson is an ex-pirate PM, and as a seafaring man I recall that so too was Sir Francis Drake!"

Jameson chose to ignore that aspect, knowing full well there was always the possibility of a recall to Special Branch at any time. He was aware that after three assignments, his cover was still unbroken, and that his shadowy code name of 'Drake' was all opponents of the West knew of him. However, as they filed out of the Prime Minister's room, Jameson could think only of the challenging prospects his new appointment offered. And it was not until they reached the open door of the Commander's car, held by the chauffeur, Wilkes, that Jameson asked:

"Did you know of this, Commander?"

The Commander shook his head. "Did I imply I had such a post in mind for you Jameson?"

Jameson could not help thinking of a certain threat made by his Commander before the Beachcomber events, but he said nothing. And Burt said nothing about the little matter yet to be finalised concerning what amounted to piracy on the high seas. If this top secret venture were to take place, doubtless mention of it would be made to him at the gala ball held at the American Embassy and to which he and Erhardt were cordially invited.

"I shouldn't think anyone knew except the old man himself. He's a shrewd politician. But what a masterly stroke!"

"Don't you think I shall be his puppet?" retorted Jameson. "As I said in there, I've got some strong views on entertainment."

"Oh, I know you well enough to know your ethical code. You will be fair."

"And besides, Commander," Jameson added with a chuckle, "being a Cabinet Minister will mean that I have a vote on all subjects, including defence."

Leanna took his arm impulsively.

"Now, now," she chided, *"no more blackmail."*

"No more blackmail indeed," agreed Commander Burt.

Although he was well aware that from the beginning of their association he had used just such a weapon against Peter Jameson.

Chapter 21

Epilogue – Piracy on the High Seas

The telephone awoke Peter Jameson from his celebration slumbers early next morning. He groaned because the time was a mere 8 a.m. and 'Horses and Carriages' for himself and Erhardt from the party they had attended at the American Embassy, had not been until 3 a.m. Burt's tones, for it was he, were conspiratorial as he informed Jameson that Wilkes was on his way to collect him for the first leg of their secret mission. In the wake of the success of Operation Beachcomber they still had to deal with the fact that there was on the high seas a Libyan fleet of tankers carrying illegal oil bound for Ireland and into the business hands of IRA sympathisers. There to be factored by them legitimately and marketed by them for profit providing funds to support their escalating terrorist campaign. The well-placed minions of the late HH's organisation had ensured contracts to supply the United States with oil requirements.

When during the course of his investigations into the deadly Irish all this came to Jameson's attention, he, having in his mind his boss's naval origins, had suggested invoking a little modern piracy which would solve the problem and greatly swell the coffers of Secure-a-World. Cunningly Jameson pointed out to Burt that Sir Francis Drake was a pirate who had even had nodding Royal Assent. "And the difference between black gold and the yellow gold of yore," Jameson said, "is only the colour." And at this he got the hearty endorsement of Allan

Dallas when it was put to him, so a plan was developed for Secure-a-World agents to secretly hi-jack the entire oil shipment.

The oil-carrying fleet sailed from Libyan waters into the Mediterranean sea in ones and twos along a coastal route, all the time making subtle external changes to its vessels, so as to slip through the overstretched inner ring of the trade embargo gunboats successfully and unimpeded. Once well into the high seas the facelifts would be completed, flags of convenience substituted for more acceptable international flags of convenience, and by that time the floating black gold fortune would be legal.

"If your code sign wasn't designated Drake," commented Burt when they'd first discussed the outlines of their plan as far back as Switzerland, "I would have recommended Robin Hood!"

Jameson shaved and dressed and kissed Leanna Erhardt a fond farewell all in the space of fifteen minutes because that was all the time he had before Wilkes pressed his apartment buzzer to signify his arrival and Jameson's departure to the Mediterranean. There was a brief meeting between Dallas, Burt and Jameson, and two naval high-rankers one American, one British, in an unknown room at Admiralty Arch, when the plans were made for the former three to be jump-jetted from RAF Northolt to the floating SAW HQ, a converted aircraft carrier in the Mediterranean.

From Secure-a-World's floating headquarters which had minesweeping attachments and all the latest electronic equipment, where it cruised permanently in the Mediterranean, Jameson's pirate operation would be shadowed.

The operation had already begun and Jameson, dressed for raiding in the mode of modern piracy, was to be the extra man of the two parties of a dozen marine commandos who were assigned to each of two motor torpedo boats. Commander Burt, with his air for the occasion, wore his slightly tight-fitting full naval uniform and Allan Dallas looked only a little out of place in his civilian clothing and the short reefer jacket he'd borrowed from Commander Burt.

Already stationed in the designated area were four enormous but empty American tankers, they were there to trans-ship the entire oil cargo after it had been hi-jacked from the Libyan fleet. Assisting in this act of legitimatised piracy were two formidable destroyers from the US navy with special orders which were top secret, with only the destroyer's commander, Allan Dallas, Commander Burt and Jameson privy to them. Pirate Jameson alone carried the sealed secret destination orders for the initiative, and the plan implemented by him at sea would be disavowed in the event of mishap. When the lengthy oil transfer operation was completed trained naval divers from the destroyers would 'time switch' limpet mines which would sink the Libyan fleet by remote control when the ships were out of sight and range.

Before all this, however, HQ's aircraft carrier shadowed them, awaiting a 'go' signal from the lead MTB that all was ready, and then HQ's mighty transmitters would jam the entire Libyan fleet's communication system, and a temporary false communications service would be substituted, seemingly coming from the oil fleet but actually being sent from the American fleet substitution. This ruse would be good enough to fool any coastguard monitoring action.

Jameson prepared to jump the final six feet from the lowered platform which had him dangling beside the converted aircraft carrier, to join the others waiting in the lead MTB. This bumped urgently against the larger vessel in the sea's swell and seemed as if it was anxious to open its powerful motors and be on its way.

"The sea's a bit frisky today, Commander," Jameson shouted to Burt way above him before he launched himself forward into an MTB and an act of daring international piracy.

"You'll soon get your sea legs young man," came back Burt's faint farewell from aloft. And then the MTB's motors were opened up and with a throaty roar Operation Sir Francis Drake was under way.

It was one of the calmer days of the winter in the Atlantic Ocean, which was where the Secure-a-World interception was planned, and as they approached their targets Jameson said to the American naval commander who had binoculars raking the Libyan tankers: "See anything unusual aboard we should know about, skipper?"

"Not really but I didn't expect a mounted machine gun." He laughed. "We never get much trouble, Pete," he said. "But they've joined up into a big fleet this time so you never know."

Jameson did know!

"I can understand why they don't offer a lot of resistance," Jameson said. "They are not warships and the crew are after all probably only merchant seamen, workers hired to do a job, aren't they?"

"The worst we usually get is a bit of a punch up, sir. But with terrorists you never know! Can't take any chances, we have to show 'em we're armed and tough! Bloody Arabs," he growled.

The American did not quite know what to make of Jameson's position in the raid, as at the briefing his status had been unclear. He chose to believe Jameson to be a sort of armed British observer and therefore viewed him with an element of mistrust. He said. "You never know for sure what you'll get when you're dealing with Middle East terrorist countries so I don't need to tell you to be watchful. But you're more'n likely right sir, we'll probably find an under-crewed bunch of sailors well past their sell by dates."

Jameson could now see with his naked eye the two destroyers gently zig-zagging fore and aft to police the Libyan vessels, but of the American tankers there was no sign. Jameson guessed, however, that they would not be far over the horizon.

The commander raised his loud hailer and spoke through it, as the signal to jam their quarry's communications system had already been given.

"This is an international operation carried out under unilateral law," he said with familiar military precision. "Commander Jones speaking. You are suspected of sanction-breaking and are therefore subject to search and arrest within my authorised jurisdiction. Heave too and prepare to be boarded. We are armed so do not offer resistance."

Without waiting for any reply the two speed boats sped into action using practised drill and ascending via hastily thrown grappling rope ladders. Soon Jameson too found himself on the deck of the first vessel. He looked about him at the men now coming from below. They looked surprised, some did not look at all like crew men. Unless they had taken to wearing suits for seamanship. Resistance they did not get, only a whipped sullenness, and the raiding party lined the assortment of men up to search them for weapons. None were found and as it would take much time to find any on a ship so full of nooks and crannies, however hastily hidden, it was decided that extreme watchfulness would be the order of the day and a party of men from a destroyer came to assist. The large American tankers appeared alongside and the transfer of oil began in earnest. Jameson now began to pay particular attention to the better dressed captives who kept themselves apart from the rest of the crew. Suits and expensive casual clothes suggested to Jameson that their presence on such an uncomfortable vessel meant there was special reason for this covert entrance into Ireland to make use of the British Government's ineffective immigration vetting which meant relatively easy access to the mainland of the United Kingdom for those thus organised. Jameson studied one man's face closely and although he had seen the face only on poor police photographs it bore a remarkable resemblance to the terrorist wanted for questioning (which meant he did it) concerning the Lockerbie aircraft bomb. The throwing knife, sheathed to his left forearm made that limb itch, and he thought of his position as judge, jury, and executioner, or the option of consigning him to the poetic justice of being blown up in the tanker. The thought intrigued him briefly but he resisted the momentary temptation and examined the man's companion closely, but his appearance rang no bells.

Many hours later with the transfer of oil approaching completion, the military leader of the raid approached the Commander in Chief. Seeking confirmation of his thoughts, Jameson decided to ask Commander Jones if the man in the white suit rang any bells with him. Commander Jones was a Welsh descendant of the Pilgrim Fathers and was an American of integrity.

"I was told you would have the final destination paperwork for me to en route our tankers sir, and orders concerning the route the empty Libyan vessels will take." As he said this his light Welshman's accent was still noticeable despite the passing of generations. Jameson withdrew the thick envelope from his inside pocket his smile matching the calm sea.

"I know is contents, Jack," he said, flipping it on his hand, "Because I helped fashion them. However, you needed it official and in writing so here it is, signed, sealed and delivered. But before you open it and disappear to study routes, I want to ask you a question. You see the guy over there in the white suit," cautiously Jameson inclined his head, a movement Jones followed only with his eyes. Remember Lockerbie...?"

"Holy godfather that's him, the one that got away. The one the Libyan's refuse to extradite, and that's his buddy. We've been instructed to watch for them and to arrest on sight. I'll...

"Steady Jack," interrupted Jameson quickly. "I feel the same... and I'm allowed to kill him legally but I do not want to jeopardise our mission for any reason and to get involved in revenge killings could do just that. There's a better way for Secure-a-World to benefit now, and we'll let someone else take care of both of them the other way, if somebody higher than me decides that is what is to be done. I shall be seeing that other person in the US next week. OK? Now these bills of lading for the oil will say that this shipment came from the North Sea!" Jameson grinned. "It did too didn't it?" he said, "And it gives as its description appropriately enough, North Sea crude." Jameson continued. "The papers will show the four American tankers routed directly from Scotland to New York. This was a considered factor when we decided to trans-ship in the Atlantic and not in the Med, where it is calmer but less private." He said. "We were lucky with the weather. Now you will despatch these six Libyan ships to the bottom of the ocean, but there is no paperwork for that. Those are the orders I have to implement, which I think will hit Gadaffi and co twice in the pocket and cost billions. Loss of oil and loss of uninsured shipping. He cannot prove he was shipping anything and there will be not a trace to prove anything was lost. Got it?"

Only Jameson and Anna Dubric knew from the Secure-a-World inside team that the shipping was owned not by Gadaffi but by Saddam Hussain the Iraqi dictator, and that half of the oil was his. This was the delicate deal that Shaheen, the oily Arab whom Anna Dubric had known from The Fanlight Club, had negotiated with O'Hara and Sweeney in London. They were all dead now and Jameson had withheld from Burt and Dallas any mention of the vital information concerning Iraqi involvement. Pirate Jameson's plan would not have withstood the full glare of the United Nations debate the situation would have warranted had it been known!

The surprise on Commander Jones' face was only momentary as, despite not being in possession of any of the true facts, he thought he saw the wisdom of the decision as he understood it. This was one of the more useful ways Government had of wasting other people's money, in his opinion. The loss of six uninsured tankers is a considerable one for any country, plus the enormous value of the pirated oil, a further loss to them and a 'spoils of war' gain to America. Billions not millions were to be made and lost on this venture!

"And Wall Street won't know a thing about this one, Jameson," he said, knowingly smiling. "Have the destroyers been briefed, sir?" He also asked.   Now a new respect for Jameson's status was apparent in his voice.

"Of course, commander, and they have been quietly going about their work during the noise of the unloading and loading. It must have been one of the divers easier jobs to operate with so much noise available to cover their activities." Replied Jameson. "The actual orders to blow I will give when we are about a hundred nautical miles away.   The destroyers going about their scheduled NATO exercises will be on hand to pick up any pieces which surface, making the operation a squeaky clean job." Jameson said, completing his explanation. "We might just about hear the bangs if sound travels as well as they say it does over water," he then said with a smile.

A scuffle broke out near at hand which looked to Jameson to be a contrived event, but Jameson's eyes had never been far from his Lockerbie suspect. He was the one man with much to fear and he needed to exchange himself for an innocent crew member.

The captain waded into the fighting men shouting. "Won't these people ever learn they can't get away," but Jameson kept his eyes on the swarthy man in the white suit. When he saw his hand delve under a tarpaulin toward which he'd moved, Jameson withdrew the throwing knife from its sheaf and threw it with unerring accuracy at the hand which was emerging gripping an automatic. The balanced throwing knife shimmied through the air and penetrated the back of the hand with a force which pinned it to the wooden deck. The pain and fear was etched into the Libyan's face and he let out a pig-like squeal. Ignoring this and the clumsy fighting taking place about him, Jameson moved in to handcuff the Libyan, wiping the blood from the knife on the man's already stained designer suit.

*

Burt, Dallas and Jameson stood on the deck of the converted aircraft carrier. They were dressed in flying gear and ready to board their respective aircraft which were to return them to RAF Northolt in England. The Lockerbie prisoners were safely installed in the bowels of the vessel, awaiting presidential instructions on prisoners he did not yet know he had. An election year bonus indeed.

"When you shake the president's hand next week Pete and he finds out your involvement in throwing him such a crock of gold, I guess they'll be even greater warmth in his handshake." Dallas said. "And where did you learn to throw a chiv like that? The ship's doctor informs me you split a tendon in the man's hand from about twenty paces."

"That is a question I would like to know the answer to, for many reasons, Allan," Burt said, half seriously, "We don't teach that in our spy schools. How did you learn to throw a knife life a circus artiste?" Burt asked.

"Ah, my secrets you would learn." Jested Jameson, but his voice was competing with the scream of the waiting aircraft's jets. "There was this sneaky Arab I encountered on a job I did for the CIA in Syria. He saved his life by teaching me the secrets of long distance carvery. He lost an ear and I got his knife.

"Now, changing the subject gents. How much of that oil money will we be able to keep for our Secure-a-World coffers?" Jameson said. "Because I think I'm due a substantial bonus – duty free!"

"Ah now that comes down to politics, Jameson," Burt said, feeling on slightly safer ground. "The president will have his own money laundering problems explaining billions coming in for oil he didn't buy." Burt said. "Say, help me out here Allan. How is he going to do that?"

"He could say he won it on the National Lottery, sir!" Said Jameson. And he put his head down and ran for the leading plane.

"And as to bonuses," shouted Burt after him. "Haven't I already had you raised to cabinet status with all that extra money!" But his words were lost in the scream of jet engines. Anyway Peter Jameson had his own methods for creating bonuses."